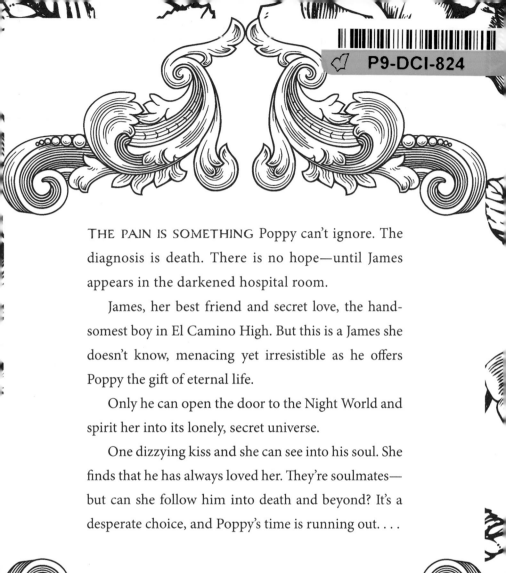

THE PAIN IS SOMETHING Poppy can't ignore. The diagnosis is death. There is no hope—until James appears in the darkened hospital room.

James, her best friend and secret love, the handsomest boy in El Camino High. But this is a James she doesn't know, menacing yet irresistible as he offers Poppy the gift of eternal life.

Only he can open the door to the Night World and spirit her into its lonely, secret universe.

One dizzying kiss and she can see into his soul. She finds that he has always loved her. They're soulmates—but can she follow him into death and beyond? It's a desperate choice, and Poppy's time is running out. . . .

NIGHT WORLD

THE NIGHT WORLD SERIES

· · · · · · · · · · · · · · · · ·

Night World

Daughters of Darkness

Spellbinder

Dark Angel

The Chosen

Soulmate

Huntress

Black Dawn

Witchlight

NIGHT WORLD · BOOK ONE

PREVIOUSLY TITLED *SECRET VAMPIRE*

L. J. SMITH

SIMON PULSE

NEW YORK   LONDON   TORONTO   SYDNEY   NEW DELHI

SIMON PULSE

An imprint of Simon & Schuster Children's Publishing Division

1230 Avenue of the Americas, New York, New York 10020

This Simon Pulse hardcover edition December 2016

Text copyright © 1996 by Lisa J. Smith

Previously titled *Secret Vampire*

Cover illustration copyright © 2016 by Neal Williams

Endpaper art of flowers, heart, and sunburst respectively copyright © 2016

by Liliya Shlapak, Nattle, and Ezepov Dmitry/Shutterstock.com

Endpaper art of ornamental flourishes copyright © 2016 by Thinkstock

All rights reserved, including the right of reproduction in whole or in part in any form.

SIMON PULSE and colophon are registered trademarks of Simon & Schuster, Inc.

NIGHT WORLD is a trademark of Lisa J. Smith

For information about special discounts for bulk purchases, please contact

Simon & Schuster Special Sales at 1-866-506-1949 or business@simonandschuster.com.

The Simon & Schuster Speakers Bureau can bring authors to your live event.

For more information or to book an event contact the Simon & Schuster Speakers Bureau

at 1-866-248-3049 or visit our website at www.simonspeakers.com.

Cover designed by Regina Flath

Interior designed by Mike Rosamilia

The text of this book was set in Adobe Garamond.

Manufactured in the United States of America

2 4 6 8 10 9 7 5 3 1

Library of Congress Control Number 2016948189

ISBN 978-1-4814-7962-2 (hc)

ISBN 978-1-4814-7963-9 (eBook)

For Marilyn Marlow,
a marvel of an agent.

And with thanks to Jeanie Danek
and the other wonderful nurses like her.

CHAPTER 1

It was on the first day of summer vacation that Poppy found out she was going to die.

It happened on Monday, the first *real* day of vacation (the weekend didn't count). Poppy woke up feeling gloriously weightless and thought, *No school.* Sunlight was streaming in the window, turning the sheer hangings around her bed filmy gold. Poppy pushed them aside and jumped out of bed—and winced.

Ouch. That pain in her stomach again. Sort of a gnawing, as if something were eating its way toward her back. It helped a little if she bent over.

No, Poppy thought. I refuse to be sick during summer vacation. I *refuse.* A little power of positive thinking is what's needed here.

Grimly, doubled over—think positive, idiot!—she made her way down the hall to the turquoise-and-gold-tiled bathroom.

At first she thought she was going to throw up, but then the pain eased as suddenly as it had come. Poppy straightened and regarded her tousled reflection triumphantly.

"Stick with me, kid, and you'll be fine," she whispered to it, and gave a conspiratorial wink. Then she leaned forward, seeing her own green eyes narrow in suspicion. There on her nose were four freckles. Four and a half, if she were completely honest, which Poppy North usually was. How childish, how—*cute!* Poppy stuck her tongue out at herself and then turned away with great dignity, without bothering to comb the wild coppery curls that clustered over her head.

She maintained the dignity until she got to the kitchen, where Phillip, her twin brother, was eating Special K. Then she narrowed her eyes again, this time at him. It was bad enough to be small, slight, and curly-haired—to look, in fact, as much like an elf as anything she'd ever seen sitting on a buttercup in a children's picture book—but to have a twin who was tall, Viking-blond, and classically handsome . . . well, that just showed a certain deliberate malice in the makeup of the universe, didn't it?

"Hello, Phillip," she said in a voice heavy with menace.

Phillip, who was used to his sister's moods, was unimpressed. He lifted his gaze from the comic section of the *L.A. Times* for a moment. Poppy had to admit that he had nice eyes: questing green eyes with very dark lashes. They were the only thing the twins had in common.

"Hi," Phillip said flatly, and went back to the comics. Not many kids Poppy knew read the newspaper, but that was Phil all over. Like Poppy, he'd been a junior at El Camino High last year, and unlike Poppy, he'd made straight As while starring on the football team, the hockey team, and the baseball team. Also serving as class president. One of Poppy's greatest joys in life was teasing him. She thought he was too straitlaced.

Just now she giggled and shrugged, giving up the menacing look. "Where's Cliff and Mom?" Cliff Hilgard was their stepfather of three years and even straighter-laced than Phil.

"Cliff's at work. Mom's getting dressed. You'd better eat something or she'll get on your case."

"Yeah, yeah . . ." Poppy went on tiptoe to rummage through a cupboard. Finding a box of Frosted Flakes, she thrust a hand in and delicately pulled out one flake. She ate it dry.

It wasn't *all* bad being short and elfin. She did a few dance steps to the refrigerator, shaking the cereal box in rhythm.

"I'm a . . . sex pixie!" she sang, giving it a foot-stomping rhythm.

"No, you're not," Phillip said with devastating calm. "And why don't you put some clothes on?"

Holding the refrigerator door open, Poppy looked down at herself. She was wearing the oversize T-shirt she'd slept in. It covered her like a minidress. "This *is* clothes," she said serenely, taking a Diet Coke from the fridge.

There was a knock at the kitchen door. Poppy saw who it was through the screen.

"Hi, James! C'mon in."

James Rasmussen came in, taking off his wraparound Ray-Bans. Looking at him, Poppy felt a pang—as always. It didn't matter that she had seen him every day, practically, for the past ten years. She still felt a quick sharp throb in her chest, somewhere between sweetness and pain, when first confronted with him every morning.

It wasn't just his outlaw good looks, which always reminded her vaguely of James Dean. He had silky light brown hair, a subtle, intelligent face, and gray eyes that were alternately intense and cool. He was the handsomest boy at El Camino High, but that wasn't it, that wasn't what Poppy responded to. It was something *inside* him, something mysterious and compelling and always just out of reach. It made her heart beat fast and her skin tingle.

Phillip felt differently. As soon as James came in, he stiffened and his face went cold. Electric dislike flashed between the two boys.

Then James smiled faintly, as if Phillip's reaction amused him. "Hi."

"Hi," Phil said, not thawing in the least. Poppy had the strong sense that he'd like to bundle her up and rush her out of the room. Phillip always overdid the protective-brother bit when James was around. "So how's Jacklyn and Michaela?" he added nastily.

James considered. "Well, I don't really know."

"You don't *know*? Oh, yeah, you always drop your girl-friends just before summer vacation. Leaves you free to maneuver, right?"

"Of course," James said blandly. He smiled.

Phillip glared at him with unabashed hatred.

Poppy, for her part, was seized by joy. Goodbye, Jacklyn; goodbye Michaela. Goodbye to Jacklyn's elegant long legs and Michaela's amazing pneumatic chest. This was going to be a wonderful summer.

Many people thought Poppy and James's relationship platonic. This wasn't true. Poppy had known for years that she was going to marry him. It was one of her two great ambitions, the other being to see the world. She just hadn't gotten around to informing James yet. Right now he still thought he liked long-legged girls with salon fingernails and Italian pumps.

"Is that a new CD?" she said, to distract him from his stare out with his future brother-in-law.

James hefted it. "It's the new Ethnotechno release."

Poppy cheered. "More Tuva throat singers—I can't *wait*. Let's go listen to it." But just then her mother walked in. Poppy's mother was cool, blond, and perfect, like an Alfred Hitchcock heroine. She normally wore an expression of effortless efficiency. Poppy, heading out of the kitchen, nearly ran into her.

"Sorry—morning!"

"Hold on a minute," Poppy's mother said, getting hold of Poppy by the back of her T-shirt. "Good morning, Phil; good morning, James," she added. Phil said good morning and James nodded, ironically polite.

"Has everybody had breakfast?" Poppy's mother asked, and when the boys said they had, she looked at her daughter. "And what about you?" she asked, gazing into Poppy's face.

Poppy rattled the Frosted Flakes box and her mother winced. "Why don't you at least put milk on them?"

"Better this way," Poppy said firmly, but when her mother gave her a little push toward the refrigerator, she went and got a quart carton of lowfat milk.

"What are you planning to do with your first day of freedom?" her mother said, glancing from James to Poppy.

"Oh, I don't know." Poppy looked at James. "Listen to some music; maybe go up to the hills? Or drive to the beach?"

"Whatever you want," James said. "We've got all summer."

The summer stretched out in front of Poppy, hot and golden and resplendent. It smelled like pool chlorine and sea salt; it felt like warm grass under her back. Three whole months, she thought. That's forever. Three months is forever.

It was strange that she was actually thinking this when it happened.

"We could check out the new shops at the Village—" she

was beginning, when suddenly the pain struck and her breath caught in her throat.

It was bad—a deep, twisting burst of agony that made her double over. The milk carton flew from her fingers and everything went gray.

CHAPTER 2

P oppy!" Poppy could hear her mother's voice, but she couldn't see anything. The kitchen floor was obscured by dancing black dots.

"Poppy, are you all right?" Now Poppy felt her mother's hands grasping her upper arms, holding her anxiously. The pain was easing and her vision was coming back.

As she straightened up, she saw James in front of her. His face was almost expressionless, but Poppy knew him well enough to recognize the worry in his eyes. He was holding the milk carton, she realized. He must have caught it on the fly as she dropped it—amazing reflexes, Poppy thought vaguely. Really amazing.

Phillip was on his feet. "Are you okay? What happened?"

"I—don't know." Poppy looked around, then shrugged, embarrassed. Now that she felt better she wished they weren't all staring at her so hard. The way to deal with the pain was to ignore it, to not think about it.

"It's just this stupid pain—I think it's gastrowhatchmacallit. You know, something I ate."

Poppy's mother gave her daughter the barest fraction of a shake. "Poppy, this is not gastroenteritis. You were having some pain before—nearly a month ago, wasn't it? Is this the same kind of pain?"

Poppy squirmed uncomfortably. As a matter of fact, the pain had never really gone away. Somehow, in the excitement of end-of-the-year activities, she'd managed to disregard it, and by now she was used to working around it.

"Sort of," she temporized. "But—"

That was enough for Poppy's mother. She gave Poppy a little squeeze and headed for the kitchen telephone. "I know you don't like doctors, but I'm calling Dr. Franklin. I want him to take a look at you. This isn't something we can ignore."

"Oh, Mom, it's *vacation*. . . ."

Her mother covered the mouthpiece of the phone. "Poppy, this is nonnegotiable. Go get dressed."

Poppy groaned, but she could see it was no use. She beckoned to James, who was looking thoughtfully into a middle distance.

"Let's at least listen to the CD before I have to go."

He glanced at the CD as if he'd forgotten it, and put down the milk carton. Phillip followed them into the hallway.

"Hey, buddy, you wait out here while she gets dressed."

James barely turned. "Get a life, Phil," he said almost absently.

"Just keep your hands off my sister, you deve."

Poppy just shook her head as she went into her room. As if James cared about seeing her undressed. *If only,* she thought grimly, pulling a pair of shorts out of a drawer. She stepped into them, still shaking her head. James was her best friend, her very best friend, and she was his. But he'd never shown even the slightest desire to get his hands on her. Sometimes she wondered if he realized she was a girl.

Someday I'm going to *make* him see, she thought, and shouted out the door for him.

James came in and smiled at her. It was a smile other people rarely saw, not a taunting or ironic grin, but a nice little smile, slightly crooked.

"Sorry about the doctor thing," Poppy said.

"No. You should go." James gave her a keen glance. "Your mom's right, you know. This has been going on way too long. You've lost weight; it's keeping you up at night—"

Poppy looked at him, startled. She hadn't told anybody about how the pain was worse at night, not even James. But— sometimes James just knew things. As if he could read her mind.

"I just know *you,* that's all," he said, and then gave her a mischievous sideways glance as she stared at him. He unwrapped the CD.

Poppy shrugged and flopped on her bed, staring at the ceiling. "Anyway, I wish Mom would let me have *one* day of

vacation," she said. She craned her neck to look at James specu-
latively. "I wish I had a mom like yours. Mine's always worrying
and trying to *fix* me."

"And mine doesn't really care if I come or go. So which is
worse?" James said wryly.

"Your parents let you have your own *apartment.*"

"In a building they own. Because it's cheaper than hiring
a manager." James shook his head, his eyes on the CD he was
putting in the player. "Don't knock your parents, kid. You're
luckier than you know."

Poppy thought about that as the CD started. She and James
both liked trance—the underground electronic sound that had
come from Europe. James liked the techno beat. Poppy loved
it because it was *real* music, raw and unpasteurized, made by
people who believed in it. People who had the passion, not
people who had the money.

Besides, world music made her feel a part of other places.
She loved the differentness of it, the alienness.

Come to think of it, maybe that was what she liked about
James, too. His differentness. She tilted her head to look at him
as the strange rhythms of Burundi drumming filled the air.

She knew James better than anyone, but there was always
something, *something* about him that was closed off to her.
Something about him that nobody could reach.

Other people took it for arrogance, or coldness, or aloof-
ness, but it wasn't really any of those things. It was just—

differentness. He was more different than any of the exchange students at school. Time after time, Poppy felt she had almost put her finger on the difference, but it always slipped away. And more than once, especially late at night when they were listening to music or watching the ocean, she'd felt he was about to tell her.

And she'd always felt that if he *did* tell her, it would be something important, something as shocking and lovely as having a stray cat speak to her.

Just now she looked at James, at his clean, carven profile and at the brown waves of hair on his forehead, and thought, He looks sad.

"Jamie, nothing's *wrong*, is it? I mean, at home, or anything?" She was the only person on the planet allowed to call him Jamie. Not even Jacklyn or Michaela had ever tried that.

"What could be wrong at home?" he said, with a smile that didn't reach his eyes. Then he shook his head dismissively. "Don't worry about it, Poppy. It's nothing important—just a relative threatening to visit. An unwanted relative." Then the smile *did* reach his eyes, glinting there. "Or maybe I'm just worried about you," he said.

Poppy started to say, "Oh, *as if*," but instead she found herself saying, oddly, "Are you really?"

Her seriousness seemed to strike some chord. His smile disappeared, and Poppy found that they were simply looking at each other, without any insulating humor between them.

Just gazing into each other's eyes. James looked uncertain, almost vulnerable.

"Poppy—"

Poppy swallowed. "Yes?"

He opened his mouth—and then he got up abruptly and went to adjust her 170-watt Tall-boy speakers. When he turned back, his gray eyes were dark and fathomless.

"Sure, if you were really sick, I'd be worried," he said lightly. "That's what friends are for, right?"

Poppy deflated. "Right," she said wistfully, and then gave him a determined smile.

"But you're not sick," he said. "It's just something you need to get taken care of. The doctor'll probably give you some antibiotics or something—with a big needle," he added wickedly.

"Oh, shut up," Poppy said. He knew she was terrified of injections. Just the thought of a needle entering her skin . . .

"Here comes your mom," James said, glancing at the door, which was ajar. Poppy didn't see how he could hear anybody coming—the music was loud and the hallway was carpeted. But an instant later her mother pushed the door open.

"All right, sweetheart," she said briskly. "Dr. Franklin says come right in. I'm sorry, James, but I'm going to have to take Poppy away."

"That's okay. I can come back this afternoon."

Poppy knew when she was defeated. She allowed her

mother to tow her to the garage, ignoring James's miming of someone receiving a large injection.

An hour later she was lying on Dr. Franklin's examining table, eyes politely averted as his gentle fingers probed her abdomen. Dr. Franklin was tall, lean, and graying, with the air of a country doctor. Somebody you could trust absolutely.

"The pain is here?" he said.

"Yeah—but it sort of goes into my back. Or maybe I just pulled a muscle back there or something. . . ."

The gentle, probing fingers moved, then stopped. Dr. Franklin's face changed. And somehow, in that moment, Poppy knew it wasn't a pulled muscle. It wasn't an upset stomach; it wasn't anything simple; and things were about to change forever.

All Dr. Franklin said was, "You know, I'd like to arrange for a test on this."

His voice was dry and thoughtful, but panic curled through Poppy anyway. She couldn't explain what was happening inside her—some sort of dreadful premonition, like a black pit opening in the ground in front of her.

"Why?" her mother was asking the doctor.

"Well." Dr. Franklin smiled and pushed his glasses up. He tapped two fingers on the examining table. "Just as part of a process of elimination, really. Poppy says she's been having pain in the upper abdomen, pain that radiates to her back, pain that's worse at night. She's lost her appetite recently, and she's lost weight. And her gallbladder is palpable—that means I can feel that it's enlarged. Now, those are symptoms of a lot of things, and a sonogram will help rule out some of them."

Poppy calmed down. She couldn't remember what a gallbladder did but she was pretty sure she didn't need it. Anything involving an organ with such a silly name couldn't be serious. Dr. Franklin was going on, talking about the pancreas and pancreatitis and palpable livers, and Poppy's mother was nodding as if she understood. Poppy didn't understand, but the panic was gone. It was as if a cover had been whisked neatly over the black pit, leaving no sign that it had ever been there.

"You can get the sonogram done at Children's Hospital across the street," Dr. Franklin was saying. "Come back here after it's finished."

Poppy's mother was nodding, calm, serious, and efficient. Like Phil. Or Cliff. Okay, we'll get this taken care of.

Poppy felt just slightly important. Nobody she knew had been to a hospital for tests.

Her mother ruffled her hair as they walked out of Dr. Franklin's office. "Well, Poppet. What have you done to your-self now?"

Poppy smiled impishly. She was fully recovered from her

earlier worry. "Maybe I'll have to have an operation and I'll have an interesting scar," she said, to amuse her mother.

"Let's hope not," her mother said, unamused.

The Suzanne G. Monteforte Children's Hospital was a handsome gray building with sinuous curves and giant picture windows. Poppy looked thoughtfully into the gift shop as they passed. It was clearly a *kid's* gift shop, full of rainbow Slinkys and stuffed animals that a visiting adult could buy as a last-minute present.

A girl came out of the shop. She was a little older than Poppy, maybe seventeen or eighteen. She was pretty, with an expertly made-up face—and a cute bandanna which didn't quite conceal the fact that she had no hair. She looked happy, round-cheeked, with earrings dangling jauntily beneath the bandanna—but Poppy felt a stab of sympathy.

Sympathy . . . and fear. That girl was *really* sick. Which was what hospitals were for, of course—for really sick people. Suddenly Poppy wanted to get her own tests over with and get out of here.

The sonogram wasn't painful, but it was vaguely disturbing. A technician smeared some kind of jelly over Poppy's middle, then ran a cold scanner over it, shooting sound waves into her, taking pictures of her insides. Poppy found her mind returning to the pretty girl with no hair.

To distract herself, she thought about James. And for some reason what came to mind was the first time she'd seen James, the day he came to kindergarten. He'd been a pale, slight boy with big gray eyes and something subtly *weird* about him that made the bigger boys start picking on him immediately. On the playground they ganged up on him like hounds around a fox—until Poppy saw what was happening.

Even at five she'd had a great right hook. She'd burst into the group, slapping faces and kicking shins until the big boys went running. Then she'd turned to James.

"Wanna be friends?"

After a brief hesitation he'd nodded shyly. There had been something oddly sweet in his smile.

But Poppy had soon found that her new friend was strange in small ways. When the class lizard died, he'd picked up the corpse without revulsion and asked Poppy if she wanted to hold it. The teacher had been horrified.

He knew where to find dead animals, too—he'd shown her a vacant lot where several rabbit carcasses lay in the tall brown grass. He was matter-of-fact about it.

When he got older, the big kids stopped picking on him. He grew up to be as tall as any of them, and surprisingly strong and quick—and he developed a reputation for being tough and dangerous. When he got angry, something almost frightening shone in his gray eyes.

He never got angry with Poppy, though. They'd remained best friends all these years. When they'd reached junior high, he'd started having girlfriends—all the girls at school wanted him—but he never kept any of them long. And he never confided in them; to them he was a mysterious, secretive bad boy. Only Poppy saw the other side of him, the vulnerable, caring side.

"Okay," the technician said, bringing Poppy back to the present with a jerk. "You're done; let's wipe this jelly off you."

"So what did it show?" Poppy asked, glancing up at the monitor.

"Oh, your own doctor will tell you that. The radiologist will read the results and call them over to your doctor's office." The technician's voice was absolutely neutral—so neutral that Poppy looked at her sharply.

Back in Dr. Franklin's office, Poppy fidgeted while her mother paged through out-of-date magazines. When the nurse said "Mrs. Hilgard," they both stood up.

"Uh—no," the nurse said, looking flustered. "Mrs. Hilgard, the doctor just wants to see you for a minute—alone."

Poppy and her mother looked at each other. Then, slowly, Poppy's mother put down her *People* magazine and followed the nurse.

Poppy stared after her.

Now, what on *earth* . . . Dr. Franklin had never done *that* before.

Poppy realized that her heart was beating hard. Not fast, just hard. Bang . . . bang . . . bang, in the middle of her chest, shaking her insides. Making her feel unreal and giddy.

Don't think about it. It's probably nothing. Read a magazine.

But her fingers didn't seem to work properly. When she finally got the magazine open, her eyes ran over the words without delivering them to her brain.

What are they talking about in there? What's going *on*? It's been so long. . . .

It kept getting longer. As Poppy waited, she found herself vacillating between two modes of thought. 1) Nothing serious was wrong with her and her mother was going to come out and laugh at her for even imagining there was, and 2) Something awful was wrong with her and she was going to have to go through some dreadful treatment to get well. The covered pit and the open pit. When the pit was covered, it seemed laughable, and she felt embarrassed for having such melodramatic thoughts. But when it was open, she felt as if all her life before this had been a dream, and now she was hitting hard reality at last.

I wish I could call James, she thought.

At last the nurse said, "Poppy? Come on in."

Dr. Franklin's office was wood-paneled, with certificates and diplomas hanging on the walls. Poppy sat down in a leather chair and tried not to be too obvious about scanning her mother's face.

Her mother looked . . . too calm. Calm with strain underneath. She was smiling, but it was an odd, slightly unsteady smile.

Oh, God, Poppy thought. Something *is* going on.

"Now, there's no cause for alarm," the doctor said, and immediately Poppy became more alarmed. Her palms stuck to the leather of the chair arms.

"Something showed up in your sonogram that's a little unusual, and I'd like to do a couple of other tests," Dr. Franklin said, his voice slow and measured, soothing. "One of the tests requires that you fast from midnight the day before you take it. But your mom says you didn't eat breakfast today."

Poppy said mechanically, "I ate one Frosted Flake."

"*One* Frosted Flake? Well, I think we can count that as fasting. We'll do the tests today, and I think it's best to admit you to the hospital for them. Now, the tests are called a CAT scan and an ERCP—that's short for something even I can't pronounce." He smiled. Poppy just stared at him.

"There's nothing frightening about either of these tests," he said gently. "The CAT scan is like an X-ray. The ERCP involves passing a tube down the throat, through the stomach, and into the pancreas. Then we inject into the tube a liquid that will show up on X-rays . . ."

His mouth kept moving, but Poppy had stopped hearing the words. She was more frightened than she could remember being in a long time.

I was just joking about the interesting scar, she thought. I don't want a *real* disease. I don't want to go to the hospital, and I don't want any tubes down my throat.

She looked at her mother in mute appeal. Her mother took her hand.

"It's no big deal, sweetheart. We'll just go home and pack a few things for you; then we'll come back."

"I have to go into the hospital *today*?"

"I think that would be best," Dr. Franklin said.

Poppy's hand tightened on her mother's. Her mind was a humming blank.

When they left the office, her mother said, "Thank you, Owen." Poppy had never heard her call Dr. Franklin by his first name before.

Poppy didn't ask why. She didn't say anything as they walked out of the building and got in the car. As they drove home, her mother began to chat about ordinary things in a light, calm voice, and Poppy made herself answer. Pretending that everything was normal, while all the time the terrible sick feeling raged inside her.

It was only when they were in her bedroom, packing mystery books and cotton pajamas into a small suitcase, that she asked almost casually, "So what exactly does he think is wrong with me?"

Her mother didn't answer immediately. She was looking down at the suitcase. Finally she said, "Well, he's not sure *anything* is wrong."

"But what does he *think*? He must think something. And he was talking about my pancreas—I mean, it sounds like he thinks there's something wrong with my pancreas. I thought he was looking at my *gallbladder* or whatever. I didn't even know that my pancreas was *involved* in this. . . ."

"Sweetheart." Her mother took her by the shoulders, and Poppy realized she was getting a little overwrought. She took a deep breath.

"I just want to know the truth, okay? I just want to have some idea of what's going on. It's my body, and I've got a right to know what they're looking for—don't I?"

It was a brave speech, and she didn't mean any of it. What she really wanted was reassurance, a promise that Dr. Franklin was looking for something trivial. That the worst that could happen wouldn't be so bad. She didn't get it.

"Yes, you do have a right to know." Her mother let a long breath out, then spoke slowly. "Poppy, Dr. Franklin was concerned about your pancreas all along. Apparently things can happen in the pancreas that cause changes in other organs, like the gallbladder and liver. When Dr. Franklin felt those changes, he decided to check things out with a sonogram."

Poppy swallowed. "And he said the sonogram was— unusual. How unusual?"

"Poppy, this is all preliminary. . . ." Her mother saw her face and sighed. She went on reluctantly. "The sonogram showed that there might be something in your pancreas. Something that shouldn't be there. That's why Dr. Franklin wants the other tests; they'll tell us for sure. But—"

"Something that shouldn't be there? You mean . . . like a tumor? Like . . . cancer?" Strange, it was hard to say the words.

Her mother nodded once. "Yes. Like cancer."

CHAPTER 3

All Poppy could think of was the pretty bald girl in the gift shop.

Cancer.

"But—but they can do something about it, can't they?" she said, and even to her own ears her voice sounded very young. "I mean—if they had to, they could take my pancreas out. . . ."

"Oh, sweetheart, *of course.*" Poppy's mother took Poppy in her arms. "I promise you; if there's something wrong, we'll do anything and everything to fix it. I'd go to the ends of the earth to make you well. You *know* that. And at this point we aren't even sure that there *is* something wrong. Dr. Franklin said that it's extremely rare for teenagers to get a tumor in the pancreas. Extremely rare. So let's not worry about things until we have to."

Poppy felt herself relax; the pit was covered again. But somewhere near her core she still felt cold.

"I have to call James."

Her mother nodded. "Just make it quick."

Poppy kept her fingers crossed as she dialed James's apartment. Please be there, please *be* there, she thought. And for once, he was. He answered laconically, but as soon as he heard her voice, he said, "What's wrong?"

"Nothing—well, everything. Maybe." Poppy heard herself give a wild sort of laugh. It wasn't exactly a laugh.

"What happened?" James said sharply. "Did you have a fight with Cliff?"

"No. Cliff's at the office. And I'm going into the hospital."

"Why?"

"They think I might have cancer."

It was a tremendous relief to say it, a sort of emotional release. Poppy laughed again.

Silence on the other end of the line.

"Hello?"

"I'm here," James said. Then he said, "I'm coming over."

"No, there's no point. I've got to leave in a minute." She waited for him to say that he'd come and see her in the hospital, but he didn't.

"James, would you do something for me? Would you find out whatever you can about cancer in the pancreas? Just in case."

"Is that what they think you have?"

"They don't know for sure. They're giving me some tests. I just hope they don't have to use any needles." Another laugh, but inside she was reeling. She wished James would say something comforting.

"I'll see what I can find on the Net." His voice was unemotional, almost expressionless.

"And then you can tell me later—they'll probably let you call me at the hospital."

"Yeah."

"Okay, I have to go. My mom's waiting."

"Take care of yourself."

Poppy hung up, feeling empty. Her mother was standing in the doorway.

"Come on, Poppet. Let's go."

James sat very still, looking at the phone without seeing it.

She was scared, and he couldn't help her. He'd never been very good at inspirational small talk. It wasn't, he thought grimly, in his nature.

To give comfort you had to have a comfortable view of the world. And James had seen too much of the world to have any illusions.

He could deal with cold facts, though. Pushing aside a pile of assorted clutter, he turned on his laptop and dialed up the Internet.

Within minutes he was using Gopher to search the National Cancer Institute's CancerNet. The first file he found was listed as "Pancreatic cancer___Patient." He scanned it.

Stuff about what the pancreas did, stages of the disease, treatments. Nothing too gruesome.

Then he went into "Pancreatic cancer___Physician"—a file meant for doctors. The first line held him paralyzed.

Cancer of the exocrine pancreas is rarely curable.

His eyes skimmed down the lines. *Overall survival rate . . . metastasis . . . poor response to chemotherapy, radiation therapy and surgery . . . pain . . .*

Pain. Poppy was brave, but facing constant pain would crush anyone. Especially when the outlook for the future was so bleak.

He looked at the top of the article again. Overall survival rate less than three percent. If the cancer had spread, less than one percent.

There must be more information. James went searching again and came up with several articles from newspapers and medical journals. They were even worse than the NCI file.

The overwhelming majority of patients will die, and die swiftly, experts say. . . . Pancreatic cancer is usually inoperable, rapid, and debilitatingly painful. . . . The average survival if the cancer has spread can be three weeks to three months. . . .

Three weeks to three months.

James stared at the laptop's screen. His chest and throat felt tight; his vision was blurry. He tried to control it, telling himself that nothing was certain yet. Poppy was being tested; that didn't mean she *had* cancer.

But the words rang hollow in his mind. He had known for some time that something was wrong with Poppy. Something was—disturbed—inside her. He'd sensed that the rhythms of her body were slightly off; he could tell she was losing sleep. And the pain—he always knew when the pain was there. He just hadn't realized how serious it was.

Poppy knows, too, he thought. Deep down, she knows that something very bad is going on, or she wouldn't have asked me to find this out. But what does she expect me to do, walk in and tell her she's going to die in a few months?

And am I supposed to stand around and watch it?

His lips pulled back from his teeth slightly. Not a nice smile, more of a savage grimace. He'd seen a lot of death in seventeen years. He knew the stages of dying, knew the difference between the moment breathing stopped and the moment the brain turned off; knew the unmistakable ghost-like pallor of a fresh corpse. The way the eyeballs flattened out about five minutes after expiration. Now, that was a detail most people weren't familiar with. Five minutes after you die, your eyes go flat and filmy gray. And then your body starts to shrink. You actually get smaller.

Poppy was so small already.

He'd always been afraid of hurting her. She looked so fragile, and he could hurt somebody much stronger if he wasn't careful. That was one reason he kept a certain distance between them.

One reason. Not the main one.

The other was something he couldn't put into words, not even to himself. It brought him right up to the edge of the forbidden. To face rules that had been ingrained in him since birth.

None of the Night People could fall in love with a human. The sentence for breaking the law was death.

It didn't matter. He knew what he had to do now. Where he had to go.

Cold and precise, James logged off the Net. He stood, picked up his sunglasses, slid them into place. Went out into the merciless June sunlight, slamming his apartment door behind him.

Poppy looked around the hospital room unhappily. There was nothing so awful about it, except that it was too cold, but . . . it was a hospital. That was the truth behind the pretty pink-and-blue curtains and the closed-circuit TV and the dinner menu decorated with cartoon characters. It was a place you didn't come unless you were Pretty Darn Sick.

Oh, come on, she told herself. Cheer up a *little*. What happened to the power of Poppytive thinking? Where's Poppyanna when you need her? Where's Mary Poppy-ins?

God, I'm even making *myself* gag, she thought.

But she found herself smiling faintly, with self-deprecating humor if nothing else. And the nurses *were* nice here, and the bed was extremely cool. It had a remote control on the side that bent it into every imaginable position.

Her mother came in while she was playing with it.

"I got hold of Cliff; he'll be here later. Meanwhile, I think you'd better change so you're ready for the tests."

Poppy looked at the blue-and-white striped seersucker hospital robe and felt a painful spasm that seemed to reach from her stomach to her back. And something in the deepest part of her said, *Please, not yet. I'll never be ready.*

James pulled his Integra into a parking space on Ferry Street near Stoneham. It wasn't a nice part of town. Tourists visiting Los Angeles avoided this area.

The building was sagging and decrepit. Several stores were vacant, with cardboard taped over broken windows. Graffiti covered the peeling paint on the cinder-block walls.

Even the smog seemed to hang thicker here. The air itself seemed yellow and cloying. Like a poisonous miasma, it darkened the brightest day and made everything look unreal and ominous.

James walked around to the back of the building. There, among the freight entrances of the stores in front, was one door unmarked by graffiti. The sign above it had no words. Just a picture of a black flower.

A black iris.

James knocked. The door opened two inches, and a skinny kid in a wrinkled T-shirt peered out with beady eyes.

"It's me, Ulf," James said, resisting the temptation to kick the door in. Werewolves, he thought. Why do they have to be so territorial?

The door opened just enough to let James in. The skinny kid glanced suspiciously outside before shutting it again.

"Go mark a fire hydrant or something," James suggested over his shoulder.

The place looked like a small café. A darkened room with little round tables crammed in side by side, surrounded by wooden chairs. There were a few scattered people sitting down, all of them looking like teenagers. Two guys were playing pool in the back.

James went over to one of the round tables where a girl was sitting. He took off his sunglasses and sat down.

"Hi, Gisèle."

The girl looked up. She had dark hair and blue eyes. Slanted, mysterious eyes which seemed to have been outlined in black eyeliner—ancient-Egyptian style.

She looked like a witch, which was no coincidence.

"James. I've missed you." Her voice was soft and husky. "How's it going these days?" She cupped her hands around the unlit candle on the table and made a quick motion as if releasing a captive bird. As her hands moved away, the candlewick burst into flame.

"Still as gorgeous as ever," she said, smiling at him in the dancing golden light.

"That goes for you, too. But the truth is, I'm here on business."

She arched an eyebrow. "Aren't you always?"

"This is different. I want to ask your . . . professional opinion on something."

She spread her slender hands, silver fingernails glowing in the candle's flame. On her index finger was a ring with a black dahlia. "My powers are at your disposal. Is there someone you want cursed? Or maybe you want to attract good luck or prosperity. I know you can't need a love charm."

"I want a spell—to cure a disease. I don't know if it needs to be specific to the disease, or if something more general would work. A—general health spell . . ."

"James." She chuckled lazily and put a hand on his, stroking lightly. "You're really worked up, aren't you? I've never seen you like this."

It was true; he was experiencing a major loss of control. He worked against it, disciplining himself into perfect stillness.

"What particular disease are we talking about?" Gisèle asked, when he didn't speak again.

"Cancer."

Gisèle threw back her head and laughed. "You're telling me your kind can get cancer? I don't believe it. Eat and breathe all you want, but don't try to convince me the lamia get human diseases."

This was the hard part. James said quietly, "The person

with the disease isn't my kind. She's not your kind, either. She's human."

Gisèle's smile disappeared. Her voice was no longer husky or lazy as she said, "An outsider? *Vermin?* Are you crazy, James?"

"She doesn't know anything about me or the Night World. I don't want to break any laws. I just want her well."

The slanted blue eyes were searching his face. "Are you sure you haven't broken the laws already?" And when James looked determined not to understand this, she added in a lowered voice, "Are you sure you're not in love with her?"

James made himself meet the probing gaze directly. He spoke softly and dangerously. "Don't say that unless you want a fight."

Gisèle looked away. She played with her ring. The candle flame dwindled and died.

"James, I've known you for a long time," she said without looking up. "I don't want to get you in trouble. I believe you when you say you haven't broken any laws—but I think we'd both better forget this conversation. Just walk out now and I'll pretend it never happened."

"And the spell?"

"There's no such thing. And if there was, I wouldn't help you. Just go."

James went.

There was one other possibility that he could think of. He drove to Brentwood, to an area that was as different from the last as a diamond is from coal. He parked in a covered carport by a quaint adobe building with a fountain. Red and purple bougainvillaea climbed up the walls to the Spanish tile on the roof.

Walking through an archway into a courtyard, he came to an office with gold letters on the door. *Jasper R. Rasmussen, Ph.D.* His father was a psychologist.

Before he could reach for the handle, the door opened and a woman came out. She was like most of his father's clients, forty-something, obviously rich, wearing a designer jogging suit and high-heeled sandals.

She looked a little dazed and dreamy, and there were two small, rapidly healing puncture wounds on her neck.

James went into the office. There was a waiting room, but no receptionist. Strains of Mozart came from the inner office. James knocked on the door.

"Dad?"

The door opened to reveal a handsome man with dark hair. He was wearing a perfectly tailored gray suit and a shirt with French cuffs. He had an aura of power and purpose.

But not of warmth. He said, "What is it, James?" in the same voice he used for his clients: thoughtful, deliberate, confident.

"Do you have a minute?"

His father glanced at his Rolex. "As a matter of fact, my next patient won't be here for half an hour."

"There's something I need to talk about."

His father looked at him keenly, then gestured to an over-stuffed chair. James eased into it, but found himself pulling forward to sit on the edge.

"What's on your mind?"

James searched for the right words. Everything depended on whether he could make his father understand. But what were the right words? At last he settled for bluntness.

"It's Poppy. She's been sick for a while, and now they think she has cancer."

Dr. Rasmussen looked surprised. "I'm sorry to hear that." But there was no sorrow in his voice.

"And it's a bad cancer. It's incredibly painful and just about one hundred percent incurable."

"That's a pity." Again there was nothing but mild surprise in his father's voice. And suddenly James knew where *that* came from. It wasn't surprise that Poppy was sick; it was surprise that James had made a trip just to tell him this.

"Dad, if she's got this cancer, she's *dying*. Doesn't that mean anything to you?"

Dr. Rasmussen steepled his fingers and stared into the ruddy gloss of his mahogany desk. He spoke slowly and steadily. "James, we've been through this before. You know that your mother and I are worried about you getting too close to Poppy. Too . . . attached . . . to her."

James felt a surge of cold rage. "Like I got too attached to Miss Emma?"

His father didn't blink. "Something like that."

James fought the pictures that wanted to form in his mind. He couldn't think about Miss Emma now; he needed to be detached. That was the only way to convince his father.

"Dad, what I'm trying to say is that I've known Poppy just about all my life. She's useful to me."

"How? Not in the obvious way. You've never fed on her, have you?"

James swallowed, feeling nauseated. Feed on Poppy? Use her like that? Even the thought of it made him sick.

"Dad, she's my friend," he said, abandoning any pretense of objectivity. "I can't just watch her suffer. I can't. I have to do something about it."

His father's face cleared. "I see."

James felt dizzy with astonished relief. "You understand?"

"James, at times one can't help a certain feeling of . . . compassion for humans. In general, I wouldn't encourage it—but you *have* known Poppy a long while. You feel pity for her suffering. If you want to make that suffering shorter, then, yes, I understand."

The relief crashed down around James. He stared at his father for a few seconds, then said softly, "Mercy killing? I thought the Elders had put a ban on deaths in this area."

"Just be reasonably discreet about it. As long as it seems to be natural, we'll all look the other way. There won't be any reason to call in the Elders."

There was a metallic taste in James's mouth. He stood and laughed shortly. "Thanks, Dad. You've really helped a lot."

His father didn't seem to hear the sarcasm. "Glad to do it, James. By the way, how are things at the apartments?"

"Fine," James said emptily.

"And at school?"

"School's over, Dad," James said, and let himself out.

In the courtyard he leaned against an adobe wall and stared at the splashing water of the fountain.

He was out of options. Out of hope. The laws of the Night World said so.

If Poppy had the disease, she would die from it.

CHAPTER 4

Poppy was staring without appetite at a dinner tray of chicken nuggets and french fries when Dr. Franklin came in the room.

The tests were over. The CAT scan had been all right, if claustrophobic, but the ERCP had been awful. Poppy could still feel the ghost of the tube in her throat every time she swallowed.

"You're leaving all this great hospital food," Dr. Franklin said with gentle humor. Poppy managed a smile for him.

He went on talking about innocuous things. He didn't say anything about the test results, and Poppy had no idea when they were supposed to come in. She was suspicious of Dr. Franklin, though. Something about him, the gentle way he patted her foot under the blanket or the shadows around his eyes . . .

When he casually suggested that Poppy's mother might

want to "come for a little walk down the hall," Poppy's suspicion crystallized.

He's going to tell her. He's got the results, but he doesn't want me to know.

Her plan was made in the same instant. She yawned and said, "Go on, Mom; I'm a little bit sleepy." Then she lay back and shut her eyes.

As soon as they were gone, she got off the bed. She watched their retreating backs as they went down the hall into another doorway. Then, in her stocking feet, she quietly followed them.

She was delayed for several minutes at the nursing station. "Just stretching my legs," she said to a nurse who looked inquiringly at her, and she pretended to be walking at random. When the nurse picked up a clipboard and went into one of the patients' rooms, Poppy hurried on down the corridor.

The room at the end was the waiting room—she'd seen it earlier. It had a TV and a complete kitchen setup so relatives could hang out in comfort. The door was ajar and Poppy approached it stealthily. She could hear the low rumble of Dr. Franklin's voice, but she couldn't hear what he was saying.

Very cautiously Poppy edged closer. She chanced one look around the door.

She saw at once that there was no need for caution. Everyone in that room was completely occupied.

Dr. Franklin was sitting on one of the couches. Beside

him was an African-American woman with glasses on a chain around her neck. She was wearing the white coat of a doctor.

On the other couch was Poppy's stepfather, Cliff. His normally perfect dark hair was slightly mussed, his rock-steady jaw was working. He had his arm around her mother. Dr. Franklin was talking to both of them, his hand on her mother's shoulder.

And Poppy's mother was sobbing.

Poppy pulled back from the doorway.

Oh, my God. I've got it.

She'd never seen her mother cry before. Not when Poppy's grandmother had died, not during the divorce from Poppy's father. Her mother's specialty was coping with things; she was the best coper Poppy had ever known.

But now . . .

I've got it. I've definitely got it.

Still, maybe it wasn't so bad. Her mom was shocked, okay, that was natural. But it didn't mean that Poppy was going to *die* or anything. Poppy had all of modern medicine on her side.

She kept telling herself this as she edged away from the waiting room.

She didn't edge fast enough, though. Before she got out of earshot, she heard her mother's voice, raised in something like anguish.

"My baby. Oh, my little girl."

Poppy froze.

And then Cliff, loud and angry: "You're trying to tell me there's *nothing*?"

Poppy couldn't feel her own breathing. Against her will, she moved back to the door.

"Dr. Loftus is an oncologist; an expert on this sort of cancer. She can explain better than I can," Dr. Franklin was saying.

Then a new voice came—the other doctor. At first Poppy could only catch scattered phrases that didn't seem to *mean* anything: adenocarcinoma, splenic venous occlusion, Stage Three. Medical jargon. Then Dr. Loftus said, "To put it simply, the problem is that the tumor has spread. It's spread to the liver and the lymph nodes around the pancreas. That means it's unresectable—we can't operate."

Cliff said, "But chemotherapy . . ."

"We might try a combination of radiation and chemotherapy with something called 5-fluorouracil. We've had some results with that. But I won't mislead you. At best it may improve her survival time by a few weeks. At this point, we're looking at palliative measures—ways to reduce her pain and improve the *quality* of the time she has left. Do you understand?"

Poppy could hear choking sobs from her mother, but she couldn't seem to move. She felt as if she were listening to some play on the radio. As if it had nothing to do with her.

Dr. Franklin said, "There are some research protocols right here in southern California. They're experimenting with immunotherapy and cryogenic surgery. Again, we're talking about palliation rather than a cure—"

"Damn it!" Cliff's voice was explosive. "You're talking about a *little girl*! How did this get to—to Stage Three—without anybody noticing? This kid was dancing all night two days ago."

"Mr. Hilgard, I'm sorry," Dr. Loftus said so softly that Poppy could barely pick up the words. "This kind of cancer is called a silent disease, because there are very few symptoms until it's very far advanced. That's why the survival rate is so low. And I have to tell you that Poppy is only the second teenager I've seen with this kind of tumor. Dr. Franklin made an extremely acute diagnosis when he decided to send her in for testing."

"*I* should have known," Poppy's mother said in a thick voice. "I should have made her come in sooner. I should have—I should have—"

There was a banging sound. Poppy looked around the door, forgetting to be inconspicuous. Her mother was hitting the Formica table over and over. Cliff was trying to stop her.

Poppy reeled back.

Oh, God, I've got to get out of here. I can't see this. I can't look at this.

She turned and walked back down the hall. Her legs moved. Just like always. Amazing that they still worked.

And everything around her was just like always. The nursing station was still decorated for the Fourth of July. Her suitcase was still on the padded window seat in her room. The hardwood floor was still solid underneath her.

Everything was the same—but how could it be? How could the walls still be standing? How could the TV be blaring in the next room?

I'm going to die, Poppy thought.

Strangely enough, she didn't feel frightened. What she felt was vastly surprised. And the surprise kept coming, over and over, with every thought being interrupted by those four words.

It's my fault because (I'm going to die) I didn't go to the doctor's sooner.

Cliff said "damn" for me (I'm going to die). I didn't know he liked me enough to swear.

Her mind was racing wildly.

Something *in* me, she thought. I'm going to die because of something that's *inside* me, like that alien in the movie. It's in me right now. Right now.

She put both hands to her stomach, then pulled up her T-shirt to stare at her abdomen. The skin was smooth, unblemished. She didn't feel any pain.

But it's in there and I'm going to die because of it. Die soon. I wonder how soon? I didn't hear them talk about that.

I need James.

Poppy reached for the phone with a feeling that her

hand was detached from her body. She dialed, thinking, *Please be there.*

But this time it didn't work. The phone rang and rang. When the answering machine came on, Poppy said, "Call me at the hospital." Then she hung up and stared at the plastic pitcher of ice water by her bedside.

He'll get in later, she thought. And then he'll call me. I just have to hang on until then.

Poppy wasn't sure why she thought this, but suddenly it was her goal. To hang on until she could talk to James. She didn't need to think about anything until then; she just had to survive. Once she talked to James, she could figure out what she was supposed to be feeling, what she was supposed to *do* now.

There was a light knock at the door. Startled, Poppy looked up to see her mother and Cliff. For a moment all she could focus on was their faces, which gave her the strange illusion that the faces were floating in midair.

Her mother had red and swollen eyes. Cliff was pale, like a piece of crumpled white paper, and his jaw looked stubbly and dark in contrast.

Oh, my God, are they going to *tell* me? They *can't*; they can't make me listen to it.

Poppy had the wild impulse to run. She was on the verge of panic.

But her mother said, "Sweetie, some of your friends are

here to see you. Phil called them this afternoon to let them know you were in the hospital, and they just arrived."

James, Poppy thought, something springing free in her chest. But James wasn't part of the group that came crowding through the doorway. It was mostly girls from school.

It doesn't matter. He'll call later. I don't have to think now.

As a matter of fact, it was impossible to think with so many visitors in the room. And that was good. It was incredible that Poppy could sit there and talk to them when part of her was farther away than Neptune, but she *did* talk and that kept her brain turned off.

None of them had any idea that something serious was wrong with her. Not even Phil, who was at his brotherly best, very kind and considerate. They talked about ordinary things, about parties and Rollerblading and music and books. Things from Poppy's old life, which suddenly seemed to have been a hundred years ago.

Cliff talked, too, nicer than he had been since the days when he was courting Poppy's mother.

But finally the visitors left, and Poppy's mother stayed. She touched Poppy every so often with hands that shook slightly. If I didn't know, I'd know, Poppy thought. She isn't acting like Mom at all.

"I think I'll stay here tonight," her mother said. Not quite managing to sound offhand. "The nurse said I can sleep on the window seat; it's really a couch for parents. I'm just trying to decide whether I should run back to the house and get some things."

"Yes, go," Poppy said. There was nothing else she could say and still pretend that she didn't know. Besides, her mom undoubtedly needed some time by herself, away from this.

Just as her mother left, a nurse in a flowered blouse and green scrub pants came in to take Poppy's temperature and blood pressure. And then Poppy was alone.

It was late. She could still hear a TV, but it was far away. The door was ajar, but the hallway outside was dim. A hush seemed to have fallen over the ward.

She felt *very* alone, and the pain was gnawing deep inside her. Beneath the smooth skin of her abdomen, the tumor was making itself known.

Worst of all, James hadn't called. How could he not call? Didn't he know she needed him?

She wasn't sure how long she could go on not thinking about It.

Maybe the best thing would be to try to sleep. Get unconscious. Then she *couldn't* think.

But as soon as she turned out the light and closed her eyes, phantoms swirled around her. Not images of pretty bald girls; skeletons. Coffins. And worst of all, an endless darkness.

If I die, I won't *be* here. Will I be anywhere? Or will I just Not Be at all?

It was the scariest thing she'd ever imagined, Not-Being.

And she was definitely thinking now, she couldn't help it. She'd lost control. A galloping fear consumed her, made her shiver under the rough sheet and thin blankets. *I'm going to die, I'm going to die, I'm going to—*

"Poppy."

Her eyes flew open. For a second she couldn't identify the black silhouette in the darkened room. She had a wild idea that it was Death itself coming to get her.

Then she said, *"James?"*

"I wasn't sure if you were asleep."

Poppy reached for the bedside button that turned on the light, but James said, "No, leave it off. I had to sneak past the nurses, and I don't want them to throw me out."

Poppy swallowed, her hands clenched on a fold of blanket. "I'm glad you came," she said. "I thought you weren't going to come." What she really wanted was to throw herself into his arms and sob and scream.

But she didn't. It wasn't just that she'd never done anything like that with him before; it was something about *him* that stopped her. Something she couldn't put her finger on, but that made her feel almost . . . frightened.

The way he was standing? The fact that she couldn't see his face? All she knew was that James suddenly seemed like a stranger.

He turned around and very slowly closed the heavy door.

Darkness. Now the only light came in through the window.

Poppy felt curiously isolated from the rest of the hospital, from the rest of the world.

And that should have been good, to be alone with James, protected from everything else. If only she weren't having this weird feeling of not recognizing him.

"You know the test results," he said quietly. It wasn't a question.

"My mom doesn't know I know," Poppy said. How could she be talking coherently when all she wanted to do was scream? "I overheard the doctors telling her. . . . James, I've got it. And . . . it's bad; it's a bad kind of cancer. They said it's already spread. They said I'm going to . . ." She couldn't get the last word out, even though it was shrieking through her mind.

"You're going to die," James said. He still seemed quiet and centered. Detached.

"I read up on it," James went on, walking over to the window and looking out. "I know how bad it is. The articles said there was a lot of pain. Serious pain."

"James," Poppy gasped.

"Sometimes they have to do surgery just to try to stop the pain. But whatever they do, it won't save you. They can fill you full of chemicals and irradiate you, and you'll still die. Probably before the end of summer."

"James—"

"It will be your last summer—"

"James, for God's sake!" It was almost a scream. Poppy was breathing in great shaking gulps, clinging to the blankets. "Why are you doing this to me?"

He turned and in one movement seized her wrist, his fingers closing over the plastic hospital bracelet. "I want you to understand that they can't help you," he said, ragged and intense. "Do you understand that?"

"*Yes*, I understand," Poppy said. She could hear the mounting hysteria in her own voice. "But is that what you came here to say? Do you want to *kill* me?"

His fingers tightened painfully. "No! I want to save you." Then he let out a breath and repeated it more quietly, but with no less intensity. "I want to save you, Poppy."

Poppy spent a few moments just getting air in and out of her lungs. It was hard to do it without dissolving into sobs. "Well, you can't," she said at last. "Nobody can."

"That's where you're wrong." Slowly he released her wrist and gripped the bed rail instead. "Poppy, there's something I've got to tell you. Something about me."

"James . . ." Poppy could breathe now, but she didn't know what to say. As far as she could tell, James had gone crazy. In a way, if everything else hadn't been so awful, she might have been flattered. James had lost his consummate cool—over her. He was upset enough about her situation to go completely nonlinear.

"You really do care," she said softly, with a laugh that

was half a sob. She put a hand on his where it rested on the bed rail.

He laughed shortly in turn. His hand flipped over to grasp hers roughly; then he pulled away. "You have no idea," he said in a terse, strained voice.

Looking out the window, he added, "You think you know everything about me, but you don't. There's something very important that you don't know."

By now Poppy just felt numb. She couldn't understand why James kept harping on himself, when *she* was the one about to die. But she tried to conjure up some sort of gentleness for him as she said, "You can tell me anything. You know that."

"But this is something you won't believe. Not to mention that it's breaking the laws."

"The law?"

"The laws. I go by different laws than you. Human laws don't mean much to us, but our own are supposed to be unbreakable."

"James," Poppy said, with blank terror. He really *was* losing his mind.

"I don't know the right way to say it. I feel like somebody in a bad horror movie." He shrugged, and said without turning, "I know how this sounds, but . . . Poppy, I'm a vampire."

Poppy sat still on the bed for a moment. Then she groped

out wildly toward the bedside table. Her fingers closed on a stack of little crescent-shaped plastic basins and she threw the whole stack at him.

"You *bastard*!" she screamed, and reached for something else to throw.

CHAPTER 5

J ames dodged as Poppy lobbed a paperback book at him.
"Poppy—"

"You jerk! You snake! How can you *do* this to me? You spoiled, selfish, immature—"

"Shhh! They're going to hear you—"

"Let them! Here I am, and I've just found out that I'm going to *die*, and all you can think of is playing a joke on me. A stupid, sick joke. I can't *believe* this. Do you think that's *funny*?" She ran out of breath to rave with. James, who had been making quieting motions with his hands, now gave up and looked toward the door.

"Here comes the nurse," he said.

"Good, and I'm going to ask her to throw you *out*," Poppy said. Her anger had collapsed, leaving her near tears. She had never felt so utterly betrayed and abandoned. "I hate you, you know," she said.

The door opened. It was the nurse with the flowered blouse and green scrub pants. "Is anything the matter here?" she said, turning on the light. Then she saw James. "Now, let's see; you don't look like family," she said. She was smiling, but her voice had the ring of authority about to be enforced.

"He's not, and I want him out of here," Poppy said.

The nurse fluffed up Poppy's pillows, put a gentle hand on her forehead. "Only family members are allowed to stay overnight," she said to James.

Poppy stared at the TV and waited for James to go. He didn't. He walked around the bed to stand by the nurse, who looked up at him while she continued straightening Poppy's blankets. Then her hands slowed and stopped moving.

Poppy glanced at her sideways in surprise.

The nurse was just staring at James. Hands limp on the blankets, she gazed at him as if she were mesmerized.

And James was just staring back. With the light on, Poppy could see James's face—and again she had that odd feeling of not recognizing him. He was very pale and almost stern looking, as if he were doing something that required an effort. His jaw was tight and his eyes—his eyes were the color of silver. Real silver, shining in the light.

For some reason, Poppy thought of a starving panther.

"So you see there's nothing wrong here," James said to the nurse, as if continuing a conversation they'd been having.

The nurse blinked once, then looked around the room as if she'd just awakened from a doze. "No, no; everything's fine," she said. "Call me if . . ." She looked briefly distracted again, then murmured, "If, um, you need anything."

She walked out. Poppy watched her, forgetting to breathe. Then, slowly, moving only her eyes, she looked at James.

"I know it's a cliché," James said. "An overused demonstration of power. But it gets the job done."

"You set this up with her," Poppy said in a bare whisper.

"No."

"Or else it's some kind of psychic trick. The Amazing Whatshisname."

"No," James said, and sat down on an orange plastic chair.

"Then I'm going *crazy*." For the first time that evening Poppy wasn't thinking about her illness. She couldn't think properly about anything; her mind was a whirling, crashing jumble of confusion. She felt like Dorothy's house after it had been picked up by the tornado.

"You're not crazy. I probably did this the wrong way; I said I didn't know how to explain it. Look, I know how hard it is for you to believe. My people *arrange* it that way; they do everything they can to keep humans not believing. Their lives depend on it."

"James, I'm sorry; I just—" Poppy found that her hands were trembling. She shut her eyes. "Maybe you'd better just—"

"Poppy, *look at me.* I'm telling you the truth. I swear it."

He stared at her face a moment, then let out a breath. "Okay. I didn't want to have to do this, but . . ."

He stood, leaning close to Poppy. She refused to flinch, but she could feel her eyes widening.

"Now, look," he said, and his lips skinned back from his teeth.

A simple action—but the effect was astonishing. Transforming. In that instant he changed from the pale but fairly ordinary James of a moment ago—into something Poppy had never seen before. A different species of human being.

His eyes flared silver and his entire face took on a predatory look. But Poppy scarcely noticed that; she was staring at his teeth.

Not teeth. Fangs. He had canines like a cat's. Elongated and curving, ending in delicate, piercing points.

They were nothing like the fake vampire fangs sold at novelty stores. They looked very strong and very sharp and very real.

Poppy screamed.

James clapped a hand over her mouth. "We don't want that nurse back in here."

When he lifted the hand, Poppy said, "Oh, my God; oh, my *God* . . ."

"All those times when you said I could read your mind," James said. "Remember? And the times when I heard things you didn't hear, or moved faster than you could move?"

"Oh, my God."

"It's true, Poppy." He picked up the orange chair and twisted one of the metal legs out of shape. He did it easily, gracefully. "We're stronger than humans," he said. He twisted the leg back and put the chair down. "We see better in the dark. We're built for hunting."

Poppy finally managed to capture an entire thought. "I don't care *what* you can do," she said shrilly. "You can't be a vampire. I've known you since you were five years *old*. And you've gotten older every year, just like me. Explain *that*."

"Everything you know is wrong." When she just stared at him, he sighed again and said, "Everything you think you know about vampires, you've picked up from books or TV. And it's all written by humans, I'll guarantee that. Nobody in the Night World would break the code of secrecy."

"The Night World. Where's the Night World?"

"It's not a place. It's like a secret society—for vampires and witches and werewolves. All the best people. And I'll explain about it later," James said grimly. "For now—look, it's simple. I'm a vampire because my parents are vampires. I was *born* that way. We're the lamia."

All Poppy could think of was Mr. and Mrs. Rasmussen with their luxury ranch-style house and their gold Mercedes. "Your *parents*?"

"*Lamia* is just an old word for vampires, but for us it means the ones who're born that way," James said, ignoring her. "We're born and we age like humans—except that we can stop aging whenever we want. We breathe. We walk around in the daylight. We can even eat regular food."

"Your parents," Poppy said again faintly.

He looked at her. "Yeah. My parents. Look, why do you think my mom does interior decorating? Not because they need the money. She meets a lot of people that way, and so does my dad, the society shrink. It only takes a few minutes alone with somebody, and the human never remembers it afterward."

Poppy shifted uncomfortably. "So you, um, drink people's blood, huh?" Even after everything she'd seen, she couldn't say it without half-laughing.

James looked at the laces of his Adidas. "Yes. Yes, I sure do," he said softly. Then he looked up and met her gaze directly.

His eyes were pure silver.

Poppy leaned back against the pile of pillows on her bed. Maybe it was easier to believe him because the unbelievable had already happened to her earlier today. Reality had already been turned upside down—so, honestly, what did one more impossibility matter?

I'm going to die and my best friend is a bloodsucking monster, she thought.

The argument was over, and she was out of energy. She and James looked at each other in silence.

"Okay," she said finally, and it meant everything she'd just realized.

"I didn't tell you this just to get it off my chest," James said, his voice still muted. "I said I could save you, remember?"

"Vaguely." Poppy blinked slowly, then said more sharply, "Save me how?"

His gaze shifted to empty air. "The way you're thinking."

"Jamie, I *can't* think anymore."

Gently, without looking at her, he put a hand on her shin under the blanket. He shook her leg slightly, a gesture of affection. "I'm gonna turn you into a vampire, kid."

Poppy put both fists to her face and began to cry.

"Hey." He let go of her shin and put an awkward arm around her, pulling her to sit up. "Don't do that. It's okay. It's better than the alternative."

"You're . . . freaking . . . crazy," Poppy sobbed. Once the tears had started, they flowed too easily—she couldn't stop them. There was comfort in crying, and in being held by James. He felt strong and reliable and he smelled good.

"You said you had to be born one," she added blurrily, between sobs.

"No, I didn't. I said *I* was born one. There are plenty of the other kind around. Made vampires. There would be more, but there's a law against just making any jerk off the street into one."

"But I *can't.* I'm just what I am; I'm *me.* I can't be—like that."

He put her gently away so he could look into her face.

"Then you're going to die. You don't have any other choice. I checked around—even asked a witch. There's nothing else in the Night World to help you. What it comes down to is: Do you want to live or not?"

Poppy's mind, which had been swamped in confusion again, suddenly fixed on this question. It was like a flashlight beam in a pitch-black room.

Did she want to live?

Oh, God, of *course* she did.

Until today she'd assumed it was her unconditional *right* to live. She hadn't even been grateful for the privilege. But now she knew it wasn't something to take for granted—and she also knew it was something she'd fight for.

Wake up, Poppy! This is the voice of reason calling. He says he can save your life.

"Wait a minute. I've got to think," Poppy said tightly to James. Her tears had stopped. She pushed him away completely and stared fiercely at the white hospital blanket.

Okay. Okay. Now get your head straight, girl.

You knew James had a secret. So you never imagined it was anything like this, so what? He's still James. He may be some godawful undead fiend, but he still cares about you. *And there's nobody else to help you.*

She found herself clutching at James's hand without looking at him. "What's it like?" she said through clenched teeth.

Steady and matter-of-fact, he said, "It's different. It's not something I'd recommend if there was another choice, but . . . it's okay. You'll be sick while your body's changing, but afterward you'll never get any kind of disease again. You'll be strong and quick—and immortal."

"I'd live forever? But would I be able to stop aging?" She had visions of herself as an immortal crone.

He grimaced. "Poppy—you'd stop aging *now*. That's what happens to made vampires. Essentially, you're *dying* as a mortal. You'll look dead and be unconscious for a while. And then . . . you'll wake up."

"I see." Sort of like Juliet in the tomb, Poppy thought. And then she thought, Oh, God . . . Mom and Phil.

"There's another thing you should know," James was saying. "A certain percentage of people don't make it."

"Don't make it?"

"Through the change. People over twenty almost never do. They don't *ever* wake up. Their bodies can't adjust to the new form and they burn out. Teenagers usually live through it, but not always."

Oddly enough, this was comforting to Poppy. A qualified hope seemed more believable than an absolute one. To live, she would have to take a chance.

She looked at James. "How do you do it?"

"The traditional way," he said with the ghost of a smile. Then, gravely: "We exchange blood."

Oh, great, Poppy thought. And I was afraid of a simple

shot. Now I'm going to have my blood drawn by fangs. She swallowed and blinked, staring at nothing.

"It's your choice, Poppy. It's up to you."

There was a long pause, and then she said, "I want to live, Jamie."

He nodded. "It'll mean going away from here. Leaving your parents. They can't know."

"Yeah, I was just realizing that. Sort of like getting a new identity from the FBI, huh?"

"More than that. You'll be living in a new world, the Night World. And it's a lonely world, full of secrets. But you'll be walking around in it, instead of lying in the ground." He squeezed her hand. Then he said very quietly and seriously, "Do you want to start now?"

All Poppy could think of to do was shut her eyes and brace herself the way she did for an injection. "I'm ready," she said through stiff lips.

James laughed again—this time as if he couldn't help it. Then he folded the bed rail down and settled beside her. "I'm used to people being hypnotized when I do this. It's weird to have you awake."

"Yeah, well, if I scream you can hypnotize me," Poppy said, not opening her eyes.

Relax, she told herself firmly. No matter how much it hurts, no matter how awful it is, you can deal with it. You *have* to. Your life depends on it.

Her heart was thumping hard enough to shake her body.

"Right here," James said, touching her throat with cool fingers as if feeling for a pulse.

Just do it, Poppy thought. Get it over with.

She could feel warmth as James leaned close to her, taking her carefully by the shoulders. Every nerve ending in her skin was aware of him. Then she felt cool breath on her throat, and quickly, before she could recoil, a double sting.

Those fangs, burying themselves in her flesh. Making two little wounds so he could drink her blood . . .

Now it's *really* going to hurt, Poppy thought. She couldn't brace herself anymore. Her life was in the hands of a hunter. She was a rabbit trapped in the coils of a snake, a mouse under the claws of a cat. She didn't feel like James's best friend, she felt like *lunch*. . . .

Poppy, what are you doing? Don't fight it. It hurts when you resist.

James was speaking to her—but the warm mouth on her throat hadn't moved. The voice was in her head.

I'm not resisting, Poppy thought. I'm just ready for it to hurt, that's all.

There was a burning where his teeth pierced her. She waited for it to get worse—but it didn't. It changed.

Oh, Poppy thought.

The feeling of heat was actually pleasant. A sensation of release, of giving.

And closeness. She and James were getting closer and closer, like two drops of water moving together until they merged.

She could sense James's mind. His thoughts—and his feelings. His emotions flowed into her, through her.

Tenderness . . . concern . . . caring. A cold black rage at the disease that was threatening her. Despair that there was no other way to help her. And longing—longing to share with her, to make her happy.

Yes, Poppy thought.

A wave of sweetness made her dizzy. She found herself groping for James's hand, their fingers intertwining.

James, she thought with wonder and joy. Her communication to him a tentative caress.

Poppy. She could feel his own surprise and delight.

And all the time the dreamy pleasure was building. Making Poppy shiver with its intensity.

How could I have been so *stupid*? Poppy thought. To be afraid of this. It isn't terrible. It's . . . right.

She had never been so close to anybody. It was as if they were one being, together, not predator and prey, but partners in a dance. Poppy-and-James.

She could touch his soul.

Strangely enough, *he* was afraid of that. She could sense it.

Poppy, don't—so many dark things—I don't want you to see . . .

Dark, yes, Poppy thought. But not dark and terrible. Dark

and lonely. Such utter loneliness. A feeling of not belonging in either of the two worlds he knew. Not belonging anywhere. Except . . .

Suddenly Poppy was seeing an image of herself. In his mind she was fragile and graceful, an emerald-eyed spirit of the air. A sylph—with a core of pure steel.

I'm not really like that, she thought. I'm not tall and beautiful like Jacklyn or Michaela. . . .

The words she heard in answer didn't seem directed toward her—she had the feeling they were something James was thinking to himself, or remembering from some long-forgotten book.

You don't love a girl because of beauty. You love her because she sings a song only you can understand. . . .

With the thought came a strong feeling of protectiveness. So this was how James felt about her—she knew at last. As if she were something precious, something to be protected at all costs. . . .

At all costs. No matter what happened to him. Poppy tried to follow the thought deeper into his mind, to find out what it meant. She got an impression of rules—no, *laws* . . .

Poppy, it's bad manners to search somebody's mind when you're not invited. The words were tinged with desperation.

Poppy pulled back mentally. She hadn't meant to pry. She just wanted to help. . . .

I know, James's thought came to her, and with it a rush of warmth and gratitude. Poppy relaxed and simply enjoyed the feeling of oneness with him.

I wish it could last forever, she thought—and just then it stopped. The warmth at her neck disappeared, and James pulled away, straightening.

Poppy made a sound of protest and tried to drag him back. He wouldn't let her.

"No—there's something else we have to do," he whispered. But he didn't do anything else. He just held her, his lips against her forehead. Poppy felt peaceful and languid.

"You didn't tell me it would be like that," she said.

"I didn't know," James said simply. "It never has been before."

They sat together quietly, with James gently stroking her hair.

So strange. Poppy thought. Everything is the same—but everything's different. It was as if she'd pulled herself up on dry land after almost drowning in the ocean. The terror that had been pounding inside her all day was gone, and for the first time in her life she felt completely safe.

After another minute or so James shook his head, rousing himself.

"What else do we have to do?" Poppy asked.

For an answer, James lifted his own wrist to his mouth. He made a quick jerking motion with his head, as if tearing a strip of cloth held in his teeth.

When he lowered the wrist, Poppy saw blood.

It was running in a little stream down his arm. So red it almost didn't look real.

Poppy gulped and shook her head.

"It's not that bad," James said softly. "And you have to do it. Without my blood in you, you won't become a vampire when you die, you'll just *die*. Like any other human victim."

And I want to live, Poppy thought. All right, then. Shutting her eyes, she allowed James to guide her head to his wrist.

It didn't taste like blood, or at least not like the blood she'd tasted when she bit her tongue or put a cut finger in her mouth. It tasted—strange. Rich and potent.

Like some magic elixir, Poppy thought dizzily. And once again she felt the touch of James's mind. Intoxicated with the closeness, she kept drinking.

That's right. You've got to take a lot, James told her. But his mental voice was weaker than it had been. Instantly Poppy felt a surge of alarm.

But what will it do to you?

"I'll be all right," James said aloud. "It's you I'm worried about. If you don't get enough, you'll be in danger."

Well, he was the expert. And Poppy was happy to let the strange, heady potion keep flowing into her. She basked in the glow that seemed to be lighting her from the inside out. She felt so tranquil, so calm. . . .

And then, without warning, the calm was shattered. A voice broke into it, a voice full of harsh surprise.

"What are you *doing*?" the voice said, and Poppy looked up to see Phillip in the doorway.

CHAPTER 6

James moved fast. He picked up the plastic tumbler on the bedside table and handed it to Poppy. She understood. Feeling giddy and uncoordinated, she took a healthy swig of water and licked her lips to wash any traces of blood away.

"What are you *doing*?" Phillip repeated, striding into the room. His eyes were fixed on James, which was good, because Poppy was trying to position herself to hide the side of her neck that James had bitten.

"None of your business," she said, and in the same instant she knew it was a mistake. Phillip, whose middle name was Stability, was looking distinctly unstable tonight.

Mom told him, Poppy thought.

"I mean, we aren't doing *anything*," she amended. It didn't help. Phil was clearly in a mood to see everything in the world as a threat to his sister. And Poppy couldn't really blame him—he'd walked in on the two of them in a strange embrace on a rumpled hospital bed.

"James was comforting me because I was scared," she said. She didn't even try to explain why James had been cradling her head to his arm. But she glanced at James's arm surreptitiously and saw that the wound there was already closed, the mark fading.

"Everything's all right, you know," James said, standing to fix a mesmerizing silver gaze on Phillip. But Phil hardly gave him a glance. He was staring at Poppy.

It's not working, Poppy thought. Maybe Phil's too mad to be hypnotized. Or too *stubborn.*

She looked a question at James, which he answered with a barely discernable shake of his head. He didn't know what the problem was, either.

But they both knew what it meant. James was going to have to leave. Poppy felt cheated and frustrated. All she wanted was to talk with James, to revel in their new discovery of each other—and she couldn't. Not with Phil here.

"How come you're here, anyway?" she asked him irritably.

"I drove Mom here. You know she doesn't like driving at night. And I brought this." He swung her boom box up onto the bedside table. "And these." He put a black CD case beside it. "All your favorite music."

Poppy felt her anger draining away. "That was sweet," she said. She was touched, especially since Phil hadn't said "All your favorite *weird* music," which was usually how he referred to it. "Thank you."

Phil shrugged, shooting a glare at James.

Poor Phil, Poppy thought. Her brother actually looked disheveled. And his eyes were swollen.

"Where's Mom?" she was starting to say, when her mother walked in.

"I'm back, sweetie," her mother said, with a very creditable cheery smile. Then she looked surprised. "James—it was nice of you to come."

"Yeah, but he was just leaving," Phil said significantly. "I'll show him the way out."

James didn't waste energy on a fight he couldn't win. He turned to Poppy and said, "I'll see you tomorrow."

There was a look in his gray eyes—gray, not silver now—that was just for her. A look that had never been there before in all the years she'd known him.

"Goodbye, James," she said softly. "And—thank you." She knew he understood what she meant.

It wasn't until he was out the door, with Phillip on his heels like a bouncer after a rowdy customer, that a thought occurred to her.

James had said that she would be in danger if she didn't get enough of his blood. But they'd gotten interrupted almost immediately after that. Had Poppy gotten enough? And what would happen if she *hadn't*?

She herself had no idea, and there was no way to ask James.

Phil stayed right behind James all the way out of the hospital.

Not tonight, James thought. He just couldn't deal with Phillip North tonight. His patience was gone, and his mind was occupied in calculating whether Poppy had taken enough of his blood to be safe. He *thought* she had—but the sooner she got more, the better.

"You'll 'see her tomorrow'—well, you're *not* going to see her tomorrow," Phil said abruptly as they walked into the garage.

"Phil, give me a break."

Instead, Phillip stepped in front of him and stopped dead, forcing James to stop, too. Phillip was breathing quickly, his green eyes burning.

"Okay, *bud*," he said. "I don't know what you think you're doing with Poppy—but it's all over now. From now on you stay away from her. *Understand?*"

Visions of breaking Phillip's neck like a new pencil danced in James's head. But Phil was Poppy's brother, and his green eyes were surprisingly like hers.

"I would never hurt Poppy," he said wearily.

"Give *me* a break. Are you going to stand there and tell me you don't want to move in on her?"

James couldn't come up with an answer immediately.

Yesterday he could have truthfully said no, he didn't want to move in on Poppy. Because it would have meant a death sentence for him and Poppy both. It was only when Poppy had received a death sentence of her own that he'd allowed himself to look at his feelings.

And now . . . now he'd been close to Poppy. He'd touched her mind, and had found that she was even braver and more gallant than he'd thought; even more compassionate—and more vulnerable.

He wanted to be that close to Poppy again. He cared about her in a way that made his throat ache. He *belonged* with Poppy.

He also realized that that might not be enough.

Sharing blood forged a powerful bond between two people. It would be wrong of him to take advantage of that bond—or of Poppy's gratitude to him. Until he was sure that Poppy's mind was clear and her decisions were her own, he should keep a little distance. It was the only honorable thing to do.

"The last thing I want to do is hurt her," he repeated. "Why can't you believe that?" He made a half-hearted attempt to capture Phil's gaze as he said it. It failed, just as it had in the hospital. Phillip seemed to be one of those rare humans who couldn't be influenced by mind control.

"Why can't I believe it? Because I *know* you. You and your—girlfriends." Phil managed to make the word sound like a curse. "You go through six or seven a year—and when you're through with them, you dump them like trash."

James was distracted briefly by amusement, because Phil was dead-on. He *needed* six girlfriends a year. After two months the bond between them became dangerously strong.

"Poppy's not my girlfriend and I'm not going to dump her," he said, pleased at his own cleverness. He'd avoided an outright lie—Poppy *wasn't* his girlfriend in any normal sense. They'd merged their souls, that was all—they hadn't talked about dating or anything.

"So you *are* telling me you're not gonna try to put the moves on her. Is that it? Because you'd better be *sure*." As he spoke, Phil did what was probably the most dangerous thing he'd ever done in his life. He grabbed James by the front of the shirt.

You stupid *human*, James thought. He briefly considered breaking every bone in Phil's hand. Or picking Phil up and throwing him across the garage into somebody's windshield. Or . . .

"You're Poppy's brother," he said through his teeth. "So I'm going to give you a chance to let go."

Phil stared into his face a moment, then let go, looking slightly shaken. But not shaken enough to keep quiet.

"You have to leave her alone," he said. "You don't understand. This disease she's got—it's serious. She doesn't need anything messing up her life right now. She just needs . . ." He stopped and swallowed.

Suddenly James felt very tired. He couldn't blame Phil for being upset—Phil's mind was full of crystal-clear pictures of Poppy dying. Usually James got only general images about what humans were thinking, but Phillip was broadcasting so loud it nearly deafened him.

Half-truths and evasions hadn't worked. It was time for Outright Lies. Anything to satisfy Phil and get James away from this.

"I know that what Poppy has is serious," he said. "I found an article about it on the Net. That's why I was *here*, okay? I feel sorry for her. I'm not interested in Poppy except as a friend, but it makes her feel better if I pretend that I like her."

Phillip hesitated, looking at him hard and suspiciously. Then he shook his head slowly. "Being friends is one thing, but it's wrong to mix her up. In the end, pretending isn't going to do her any good. I don't even think it makes her feel better *now*—she looked pretty bad in there."

"Bad?"

"Pale and shaky. You know Poppy; you know how she gets overexcited about things. You shouldn't be fooling around with her emotions." He narrowed his eyes and said, "So maybe you'd better stay away from her for a while. Just to make sure she hasn't got the wrong idea."

"Whatever," James said. He wasn't really listening.

"Okay," Phillip said. "We have a deal. But I'm warning you, if you break it, you're in trouble."

James wasn't listening to that, either. Which was a mistake.

In the darkened hospital room Poppy lay and listened to her mother's breathing.

You're not asleep, she thought, and I'm not asleep. And you know I'm not, and I know you're not. . . .

But they couldn't talk. Poppy wanted desperately to let her mother know that everything was going to be all right—but *how*? She couldn't betray James's secret. And even if she could, her mother wouldn't believe her.

I have to find a way, Poppy thought. *I have to.* And then a great wave of drowsiness overtook her. It had been the longest day in her life, and she was full of alien blood already working its strange magic in her. She couldn't . . . she just couldn't . . . keep her eyes open.

Several times during the night a nurse came in to take her vital signs, but Poppy never really woke up. For the first time in weeks, no pain interrupted her dreams.

She opened her eyes the next morning feeling confused and weak. Black dots swarmed through her vision when she sat up.

"Hungry?" her mother asked. "They left this breakfast tray for you."

The smell of hospital eggs made Poppy feel nauseated. But because her mother was watching her anxiously, she played with the food on the tray before she went to wash up. In the bathroom mirror she examined the side of her neck. Amazing—there was no trace of a mark.

When she came out of the bathroom, her mother was crying.

Not floods of tears, not sobbing. Just dabbing her eyes on a Kleenex. But Poppy couldn't stand it.

"Mom, if you're worried about telling me . . . I know."

The whole sentence was out before Poppy could even think about it.

Her mother's head jerked up in horror. She stared at Poppy with more tears spilling. "Sweetheart—you know . . . ?"

"I know what I've got and I know how bad it is," Poppy said. If this was the wrong strategy, it was too late now. "I listened when you and Cliff were talking to the doctors."

"Oh, my *Lord*."

What can I *say?* Poppy wondered. It's okay, Mom, because I'm not going to die; I'm going to become a vampire. I hope. I can't be sure, because sometimes you don't make it through the transformation. But with any luck, I should be sucking blood in a few weeks.

Come to think of it, she hadn't asked James exactly how long it would take to change her.

Her mother was taking deep, calming breaths. "Poppy, I want you to know how much I love you. Cliff and I will do anything—*anything*—we can to help you. Right now he's looking into some clinical protocols—those are experimental studies where they test new ways of treating people. If we can just . . . buy time . . . until a cure . . ."

Poppy couldn't stand it. She could *feel* her mother's pain. Literally. It came in palpable waves that seemed to echo through her bloodstream, making her dizzy.

It's that blood, she thought. It's doing something to me— changing me.

Even as she thought it, she went to her mother. She wanted to hug her, and she needed help standing up.

"Mom, I'm not scared," she said, muffled against her mother's shoulder. "I can't explain, but I'm not scared. And I don't want you to be unhappy over me."

Her mother just held on fiercely, as if Death might try to snatch Poppy out of her arms that minute. She was crying.

Poppy cried, too. Real tears, because even if she wasn't going to die truly, she was going to lose so much. Her old life, her family, everything familiar. It felt good to cry over it; it was something she needed to do.

But when it was done, she tried again.

"The *one* thing I don't want is for you to be unhappy or worry," she said, and looked up at her mother. "So could you just try not to? For my sake?"

Oh, God, I'm coming off like Beth in *Little Women*, she thought. Saint Poppy. And the truth is, if I were really dying, I'd go kicking and screaming all the way.

Still, she'd managed to comfort her mother, who drew back looking tearstained but quietly proud. "You're really something, Poppet," was all she said, but her lips trembled.

Saint Poppy looked away, horribly embarrassed—until another wave of dizziness saved her. She allowed her mother to help her back into bed.

And it was then that she finally found a way to pose the question she needed to ask.

"Mom," she said slowly, "what if there was a cure for me somewhere—like in some other country or something—and I could go there and get better, but they wouldn't ever let me come back? I mean, you'd know I was okay, but you wouldn't ever be able to see me again." She looked at her mother intently. "Would you want me to do it?"

Her mother answered instantly. "Sweetheart, I'd want you cured if you had to go to the moon. As long as you were happy." She had to pause a moment, then resumed steadily. "But, honey, there isn't such a place. I wish there were."

"I know." Poppy patted her arm gently. "I was just asking. I love you, Mom."

Later that morning Dr. Franklin and Dr. Loftus came by. Facing them wasn't as horrible as Poppy expected, but she felt like a hypocrite when they marveled over her "wonderful attitude." They talked about quality time, and the fact that no two cases of cancer were the same, and about people they'd known who'd beaten the percentages. Saint Poppy squirmed inside, but she listened and nodded—until they began to talk about more tests.

"We'd like to do an angiogram and a laparotomy," Dr. Loftus said. "Now an angiogram is—"

"Tubes stuck in my *veins*?" Poppy said before she could help herself.

Everyone looked startled. Then Dr. Loftus gave a rueful smile. "Sounds like you've been reading up on it."

"No, I just—I guess I remember it from somewhere," Poppy said. She knew where she was getting the images—from Dr. Loftus's head. And she probably should cover her tracks instead of talking anymore, but she was too distressed. "And a laparotomy's an operation, right?"

Dr. Loftus and Dr. Franklin exchanged glances. "An exploratory operation, yes," Dr. Franklin said.

"But I don't *need* those tests, do I? I mean, you already know what I've got. And the tests *hurt*."

"Poppy," her mother said gently. But Dr. Loftus was answering slowly.

"Well, sometimes we need the tests to confirm a diagnosis. But in your case . . . no, Poppy. We don't really need them. We're already sure."

"Then I don't see why I have to have them," Poppy said simply. "I'd rather go home."

The doctors looked at each other, then at Poppy's mother. Then, without even trying to be subtle about it, the three adults went out into the corridor to deliberate.

When they came back, Poppy knew she'd won.

"You can go home, Poppy," Dr. Franklin said quietly. "At least until you develop any further symptoms. The nurse will tell your mother what to look out for."

The first thing Poppy did was call James. He answered on the first ring and said, "How do you feel?"

"Dizzy. But pretty good," Poppy said, whispering because her mother was outside talking to a nurse. "I'm coming home."

"I'll come over this afternoon," James said. "Call me when you think you'll have an hour or so alone. And, Poppy . . . don't tell Phil I'm coming."

"Why not?"

"I'll explain later."

When she actually got home, it was strange. Cliff and Phil were there. Everybody was unusually nice to her, while still trying to pretend that nothing unusual was going on. (Poppy had heard the nurse tell her mother that it was good to try and maintain a normal routine.)

It's like my birthday, Poppy thought dazedly. Like some terribly important birthday and graduation rolled into one. Every few minutes the doorbell would ring as another flower arrangement arrived. Poppy's bedroom looked like a garden.

She felt badly for Phil. He looked so stricken—and so brave. She wanted to comfort him the way she'd comforted her mother—but *how*?

"Come here," she ordered, opting for direct action. And when he obeyed, she hugged him tightly.

"You'll beat this thing," he whispered. "I know you will. Nobody's ever had as much will to live as you do. And nobody's ever, *ever* been as stubborn."

It was then that Poppy realized just how terribly she was going to miss him.

When she let go, she felt light-headed.

"Maybe you'd better lie down," Cliff said gently. And Poppy's mother helped her to the bedroom.

"Does Dad know?" she asked as her mother moved around the bedroom, straightening things.

"I tried to get hold of him yesterday, but the people at the station said he'd moved to somewhere in Vermont. They don't know where."

Poppy nodded. It sounded like her dad—always on the move. He was a DJ—when he wasn't being an artist or a stage magician. He'd split up with her mom because he wasn't very good at being any of those things—or at least not good enough to get paid much.

Cliff was everything Poppy's father wasn't: responsible, disciplined, hardworking. He fit in perfectly with Poppy's mom and Phil. So perfectly that sometimes Poppy felt like the odd one out in her own family.

"I miss Dad," Poppy said softly.

"I know. Sometimes I do, too," her mother said, surprising

her. Then she said firmly, "We'll find him, Poppy. As soon as he hears, he'll want to come."

Poppy hoped so. She didn't suppose she'd get a chance to see him—after.

It wasn't until an hour or so before dinnertime, when Phil and Cliff were out doing errands, and her mother was taking a nap, that Poppy got the chance to call James.

"I'll come right over," he said. "I'll let myself in." Ten minutes later he walked into Poppy's bedroom.

Poppy felt strangely shy. Things had changed between her and James. They weren't simply best friends anymore.

They didn't even say "Hi" to each other. As soon as he came in, their eyes caught and met. And then, for an endless moment, they just looked at each other.

This time, when Poppy felt the quick pang in her chest that always came when she saw James, it was a throb of pure sweetness. He cared about her. She could see it in his eyes.

Wait a minute, hang on, her mind whispered. Don't jump the gun here. He *cares* about you, yes, but he didn't say he was *in love* with you. There's a difference.

Shut up, Poppy told her brain soberly. Aloud, she said, "How come you didn't want Phil to know you were here?"

James threw his light windbreaker over a chair and sat down on Poppy's bed. "Well—I just didn't want to be interrupted," he said with a gesture of dismissal. "How's the pain?"

"It's *gone*," Poppy said. "Isn't that weird? It didn't wake me up at all last night. And there's something else. I think I'm starting to—well, read people's thoughts."

James smiled slightly, just one corner of his mouth up. "That's good. I was worried—" He broke off and went to turn Poppy's CD player on. Plaintive Bantu wailings emerged.

"I was worried you didn't get enough blood last night," James said quietly, resuming his seat. "You'll have to take more this time—and so will I."

Poppy felt something tremble inside her. Her revulsion was gone. She was still afraid, but that was only because of the consequences of what they were going to do. It wasn't just a way to get closer or to feed James. They were doing it to *change* Poppy.

"The only thing I don't understand is why you never bit me before." Her tone was light, but as she spoke the words, she realized that there was a serious question behind them.

"I mean," she said slowly, "you did it with Michaela and Jacklyn, didn't you? And with other girls?"

He looked away but answered steadily. "I didn't exchange blood with them. But I fed on them, yes."

"But not me."

"No. How can I explain?" He looked up at her. "Poppy, taking blood can be a lot of different things—and the Elders don't want it to be anything but feeding. They say all you should feel is the joy of the hunt. And that's all I ever *have* felt—before."

Poppy nodded, trying to feel satisfied with this. She didn't ask who the Elders were.

"Besides, it can be *dangerous*," James said. "It can be done with hatred, and it can kill. Kill permanently, I mean."

Poppy was almost amused by this. "*You* wouldn't kill."

James stared at her. Outside, it was cloudy and the light in Poppy's bedroom was pale. It made James's face look pale, too, and his eyes silver.

"But I have," James said. His voice was flat and bleak. "I've killed without exchanging enough blood, so the person didn't come back as a vampire."

CHAPTER 7

Then you must have had a reason," Poppy said flatly. When he looked at her, she shrugged. "I know you." She knew him in a way she'd never known anyone.

James looked away. "I didn't have a reason, but there were some . . . extenuating circumstances. You could say I was set up. But I still have nightmares."

He sounded so tired—so sad. *It's a lonely world, full of secrets,* Poppy thought. And he'd had to keep the biggest secret of all from everyone, including her.

"It must have been awful for you," she said, hardly aware that she was speaking out loud. "I mean, all your life—holding this in. Not telling anybody. Pretending . . ."

"Poppy." He gave a shiver of repressed emotion. "Don't."

"Don't sympathize with you?"

He shook his head. "Nobody's ever understood before."

After a pause he said, "How can you worry about *me*? With what you're facing?"

"I guess because—I care about you."

"And I guess that's why I didn't treat you like Michaela or Jacklyn," he said.

Poppy looked at the sculpted planes of his face, at the wave of brown hair falling over his forehead like silk . . . and held her breath. Say "I love you," she ordered mentally. *Say it,* you thickheaded male.

But they weren't connected, and James didn't give the slightest sign of having heard. Instead he turned brisk and businesslike. "We'd better get started." He got up and drew the window curtains shut. "Sunlight inhibits all vampire powers," he said in a guest lecturer voice.

Poppy took advantage of the pause to go to the CD player. The music had changed to a Dutch club song, which was fine for doing the Netherlands skippy dance to, but not very romantic. She punched a button and a velvety Portuguese lament began.

Then she twitched the sheer hangings around the bed closed. When she sat down again, she and James were in their own little world, dim and secluded, enclosed in misty eggshell white.

"I'm ready," she said softly, and James leaned in close to her. Even in the semidarkness Poppy felt mesmerized by his eyes. They were like windows to some other place, someplace distant and magical.

The Night World, she thought, and tilted her chin back as James took her in his arms.

This time the double sting at her neck hurt good.

But best was when James's mind touched hers. The feeling of oneness, of suddenly being whole—it spread through her like starshine.

Once again she had the sense that they were melting together, dissolving and merging everywhere they touched. She could feel her own pulse echoing through him.

Closer, closer . . . and then she felt a pulling-back.

James? What's wrong?

Nothing, he told her, but Poppy could sense that it wasn't quite true. He was trying to weaken the growing bond between them . . . but why?

Poppy, I just don't want to force you into anything. What we're feeling is—artificial. . . .

Artificial? It was the realest thing that she'd ever experienced. Realer than real. In the midst of joy, Poppy felt a surge of hurt anger at James.

I don't mean it like that, he said, and there was desperation in the thought. *It's just that you can't resist the blood-bond. You couldn't resist it if you hated me. It isn't fair. . . .*

Poppy didn't care about fair. *If you can't resist it, why are you trying?* she asked him triumphantly.

She heard something like mental laughter, and then they were both clinging together as a wave of pure emotion swept them.

The blood-bond, Poppy thought when James raised his head at last. It doesn't matter if he won't say he loves me—we're bonded now. Nothing can change that.

And in a moment or so she would seal that bond by taking his blood. Try and resist *that*, she thought, and was startled when James laughed softly.

"Reading my mind again?"

"Not exactly. You're projecting—and you're very good at it. You're going to be a strong telepath."

Interesting . . . but right now Poppy didn't feel strong. She suddenly felt kitten-weak. Limp as a wilting flower. She needed . . .

"I know," James whispered. Still supporting her, he started to lift one wrist to his mouth.

Poppy stopped him with a restraining hand. "James? How many times do we have to do this before I—change?"

"Once more, I think," James said quietly. "I took a lot this time, and I want you to do the same. And the next time we do it . . ."

I'll die, Poppy thought. Well, at least I know how long I have left as a human.

James's lips slid back to reveal long, delicate fangs, and he struck at his own wrist. There was something snakelike in the motion. Blood welled up, the color of syrup in a can of cherry preserves.

Just as Poppy was leaning forward, lips parted, there was a knock at the door.

Poppy and James froze guiltily.

The knock came again. In her muddled and weakened state, Poppy couldn't seem to make herself move. The only thought that resounded in her brain was *Oh, please. Please don't let it be* . . .

The door opened.

. . . *Phil.*

Phillip was already speaking as he poked his head in. "Poppy, are you awake? Mom says—"

He broke off abruptly, then lunged for the lightswitch on the wall. Suddenly the room was illuminated.

Oh, *terrific.* Poppy thought in frustration. Phil was peering through the filmy draperies around the bed. Poppy peered back at him.

"What—is going—*on?*" he said in a voice that would have gotten him the lead role in *The Ten Commandments.* And then, before Poppy could gather enough wits to answer, he leaned in and grabbed James by the arm.

"Phil, *don't,*" Poppy said. "Phil, you idiot . . ."

"We had a deal," Phil snarled at James. "And you broke it."

James was gripping Phil's arms now, as ungently as Phil was grasping him. Poppy had the dismayed feeling that they were going to start head-butting each other.

Oh, Lord, if she could only *think* straight. She felt so brainless.

"You've got the wrong idea," James said to Phil through clenched teeth.

"The wrong *idea*? I come in here and find the two of you in bed, with all the curtains drawn, and you're telling me I've got the wrong *idea*?"

"*On* the bed," Poppy interjected. Phil ignored her.

James shook Phil. He did it quite easily and with an economy of movement, but Phil's head snapped back and forth. Poppy realized that James was not at his most rational right now. She remembered the meted chair leg and decided it was time to intervene.

"Let *go*," she said, reaching in between the two boys to grab for hands. Anybody's hands. "Come on, you guys!" And then, desperately, "Phil, I know you don't understand, but James is trying to *help* me—"

"Help you? I don't think so." And then to James: "Look at her. Can't you see that this stupid pretending is making her *sicker*? Every time I find her with you, she's white as a sheet. You're just making things worse."

"You don't know anything about it," James snarled in Phil's face. But Poppy was still processing something several sentences back.

"Stupid? Pretending?" she said. Her voice wasn't very loud but everything stopped.

Both boys looked at her.

Everyone made mistakes then. Later, Poppy would realize that if any of them had kept their heads, what happened next could have been avoided. But none of them did.

"I'm sorry," Phil said to Poppy. "I didn't want to tell you—"

"*Shut up,*" James said savagely.

"But I have to. This—*jerk*—is just playing with you. He admitted it to me. He said he felt sorry for you, and he thinks that pretending he likes you makes you feel better. He's got an ego that would fill Dodger Stadium."

"Pretending?" Poppy said again, sitting back. There was a buzzing in her head and an eruption gathering in her chest.

"Poppy, he's crazy," James said. "Listen—"

But Poppy wasn't listening. The problem was that she could *feel* how sorry Phil was. It was much more convincing than anger. And Phillip, honest, straightforward, trustworthy Phillip, almost never lied.

He wasn't lying now. Which meant . . . that James must be. Eruption time.

"You . . ." she whispered to James. "You . . ." She couldn't think of a swear word bad enough. Somehow she felt more hurt, more betrayed than she had ever felt before. She had thought she *knew* James; she had trusted him absolutely. Which made the betrayal all the worse. "So it was all pretending? Is that it?"

Some inner voice was telling her to hold on and *think*. That she was in no state to make crucial decisions. But she was also in no state to listen to inner voices. Her own anger kept her from deciding if she had any good reason to be angry.

"You just felt *sorry* for me?" she whispered, and suddenly all the fury and grief that she'd been suppressing for the last day and a half flooded out. She was blind with pain, and nothing mattered except making James hurt as much as she hurt.

James was breathing hard, speaking rapidly. "Poppy—this is why I didn't want Phil to know—"

"And no *wonder*," Poppy raged. "And no wonder you wouldn't say you loved me," she went on, not even caring that Phillip was listening. "And no wonder you would do all that other stuff, but you never even kissed me. Well, I don't want your *pity*—"

"*What other stuff? All what other stuff?*" Phil shouted. "*I'm gonna kill you, Rasmussen!*"

He tore free of James and swung at him. James ducked so that the fist just grazed his hair. Phil swung again and James twisted sideways and grabbed him from behind in a headlock.

Poppy heard running footsteps in the hall. "What's happening?" her mother gasped in dismay, regarding the scene in Poppy's bedroom.

At almost the same instant Cliff appeared behind Poppy's mother. "What's all the shouting?" he asked, his jaw particularly square.

"*You're* the one who's putting her in danger," James was snarling in Phillip's ear. "Right now." He looked feral. Savage. Inhuman.

"Let go of my *brother*!" Poppy yelled. All at once her eyes were swimming with tears.

"Oh, my God—darling," her mother said. In two steps

she was beside the bed and holding Poppy. "You boys get *out* of here."

The savagery drained out of James's expression, and he loosened his hold on Phillip. "Look, I'm sorry. I have to stay. Poppy . . ."

Phillip slammed an elbow into his stomach.

It might not have hurt James as much as it would a human, but Poppy saw the fury sweep over his face as he straightened from doubling up. He lifted Phil off his feet and threw him headfirst in the general direction of Poppy's dresser.

Poppy's mother let out a cry. Cliff jumped in between Phil and James.

"That's enough!" he roared. Then, to Phil: "Are you all right?" And to James: "What's this all about?"

Phil was rubbing his head dazedly. James said nothing. Poppy couldn't speak.

"All right, it doesn't matter," Cliff said. "I guess everybody's a little jumpy right now. But you'd better go on home, James."

James looked at Poppy.

Poppy, throbbing all over like an aching tooth, turned her back on him. She burrowed into her mother's embrace.

"I'll be back," James said quietly. It might have been meant as a promise, but it sounded like a threat.

"Not for a while, you won't," Cliff said in a military command voice. Gazing over her mother's arm, Poppy could see that there was blood on Phillip's blond hair. "I think everybody needs a cooling-off period. Now, come on, move."

He led James out. Poppy sniffled and shivered, trying to ignore both the waves of giddiness that swept over her and the agitated murmuring of all the voices in her head. The stereo went on blasting out madcore stomping music from England.

In the next two days James called eight times.

Poppy actually picked up the phone the first time. It was after midnight when her private line rang, and she responded automatically, still half-asleep.

"Poppy, don't hang up," James said.

Poppy hung up. A moment later the phone rang again.

"Poppy, if you don't want to die, you've got to listen to me."

"That's blackmail. You're *sick*," Poppy said, clutching the handset. Her tongue felt thick and her head ached.

"It's just the truth. Poppy, listen. You didn't take any blood today. I weakened you, and you didn't get anything in exchange. And that could *kill* you."

Poppy heard the words, but they didn't seem real. She found herself ignoring them, retreating into a foggy state where thought was impossible. "I don't care."

"You *do* care, and if you could think, you'd know that. It's the change that's doing this. You're completely messed up mentally. You're too paranoid and illogical and crazy to *know* you're paranoid and illogical and crazy."

It was suspiciously like what Poppy had realized earlier. She was aware, dimly, that she was acting the way Marissa Schaffer had after drinking a six-pack of beer at Jan Nedjar's New Year's party. Making a ranting fool of herself. But she couldn't seem to stop.

"I just want to know one thing," she said. "Is it true that you said that stuff to Phillip?"

She heard James let his breath out. "It's true that I said it. But what I *said* wasn't true. It was just to get him off my back."

By now Poppy was too upset to even want to calm down.

"Why should I believe somebody whose whole life is a lie?" she said, and hung up again as the first tears spilled.

All the next day she stayed in her state of foggy denial. Nothing seemed real, not the fight with James, not James's warning, and not her illness. Especially not her illness. Her mind found a way to accept the special treatment she was getting from everyone without dwelling on the reason for the treatment.

She even managed to disregard her mother's whispered comments to Phil about how she was going downhill so fast. How poor Poppy was getting pale, getting weak, getting worse. And only Poppy knew that she could now hear conversations held in the hallway as clearly as if they were in her own room.

All her senses were sharpened, even as her mind was dulled. When she looked at herself in the mirror, she was startled by how white she was, her skin translucent as candle wax. Her eyes so green and fierce that they burned.

The other six times James called, Poppy's mother told him Poppy was resting.

Cliff fixed the broken trim on Poppy's dresser. "Who would have thought the kid was that strong?" he said.

James flipped his cellular phone shut and banged a fist on the Integra's dashboard. It was Thursday afternoon.

I love you. That's what he should have said to Poppy. And now it was too late—she wouldn't even talk to him.

Why *hadn't* he said it? His reasons seemed stupid now. So he hadn't taken advantage of Poppy's innocence and gratitude . . . well, bravo. All he'd done was tap her veins and break her heart.

All he'd done was hasten her death.

But there wasn't time to think about it now. Right now he had a masquerade to attend.

He got out of the car and gave his windbreaker a twitch as he walked toward the sprawling ranch-style house.

He unlocked and opened the door without calling to announce his presence. He didn't need to announce it; his mother would sense him.

Inside, it was all cathedral ceilings and fashionably bare walls. The one oddity was that every one of the many skylights was covered with elegant custom-made drapes. This made the interior seem spacious but dim. Almost—cavernous.

"James," his mother said, coming from the back wing. She had jet-black hair with a sheen like lacquer and a perfect figure that was emphasized rather than disguised by her silver-and-gold embroidered wrap. Her eyes were cool gray and heavily lashed, like James's. She kissed the air beside his cheek.

"I got your message," James said. "What do you want?"

"I'd really rather wait until your father gets home. . . ."

"Mom, I'm sorry, but I'm in a hurry. I've got things to do—I haven't even fed today."

"It shows," his mother said. She regarded him for a moment without blinking. Then she sighed, turning toward the living room. "At least, let's sit down. . . . You've been a little agitated, haven't you, these last few days?"

James sat on the crimson-dyed suede couch. Now was the test of his acting ability. If he could get through the next minute without his mother sensing the truth, he'd be home free.

"I'm sure Dad told you why," he said evenly.

"Yes. Little Poppy. It's very sad, isn't it?" The shade of the single treelike floor lamp was deep red, and ruby light fell across half his mother's face.

"I was upset at first, but I'm pretty much over it now," James said. He kept his voice dull and concentrated on sending nothing—*nothing*—through his aura. He could feel his mother lightly probing the edges of his mind. Like an insect gently caressing with an antenna, or a snake tasting the air with its black forked tongue.

"I'm surprised," his mother said. "I thought you liked her."

"I did. But, after all, they're not really *people*, are they?" He considered a moment, then said, "It's sort of like losing a pet. I guess I'll just have to find another one."

It was a bold move, quoting the party line. James willed every muscle to stay relaxed as he felt the thought-tendrils tighten suddenly, coiling around him, looking for a chink in his armor. He thought very hard—about Michaela Vasquez. Trying to project just the right amount of negligent fondness.

It worked. The probing tendrils slipped away from his mind, and his mother settled back gracefully and smiled.

"I'm glad you're taking it so well. But if you ever feel that you'd like to talk to someone . . . your father knows some very good therapists."

Vampire therapists, she meant. To screw his head on straight about how humans were just for feeding on.

"I know you want to avoid trouble as much as I do," she added. "It reflects on the family, you see."

"Sure," James said, and shrugged. "I've got to go now. Tell Dad I said hi, okay?"

He kissed the air beside her cheek.

"Oh, by the way," she said as he turned toward the door. "Your cousin Ash *will* be coming next week. I think he'd like to stay with you at the apartment—and I'm sure you'd like some company there."

Over my unbreathing body, James thought. He'd forgotten

all about Ash's threat to visit. But now wasn't the time to argue. He walked out feeling like a juggler with too many balls in the air.

Back in his car he picked up the cellular phone, hesitated, then snapped it shut without turning it on. Calling wasn't any good. It was time to change his strategy.

All right, then. No more half measures. A serious offensive—aimed where it would do the most good.

He thought for a few minutes, then drove to McDonnell Drive, parking just a few houses away from where Poppy lived.

And then he waited.

He was prepared to sit there all night if necessary, but he didn't have to. Just around sunset the garage door opened and a white Volkswagen Jetta backed out. James saw a blond head in the driver's seat.

Hi, Phil. Nice to see you.

When the Jetta pulled away, he followed it.

CHAPTER 8

When the Jetta turned into the parking lot of a 7-Eleven, James smiled. There was a nice isolated area behind the store, and it was getting dark.

He drove his own car around back, then got out to watch the store entrance. When Phil came out with a bag, he sprang on him from behind.

Phil yelled and fought, dropping the bag. It didn't matter. The sun had gone down and James's power was at full strength.

He dragged Phil to the back of the store and put him facing the wall beside a Dumpster. The classic police frisking position.

"I'm going to let go now," he said. "Don't try to run away. That would be a mistake."

Phil went tense and motionless at the sound of his voice.

"I don't *want* to run away. I want to smash your face in, Rasmussen."

"Go ahead and try." James was going to add, *Make my night,* but he reconsidered. He let go of Phil, who turned around and regarded him with utter loathing.

"What's the matter? Run out of girls to jump?" he said, breathing hard.

James gritted his teeth. Trading insults wasn't going to do any good, but he could already tell it was going to be hard to keep his temper. Phil had that effect on him. "I didn't bring you out here to fight. I brought you to ask you something. Do you care about Poppy?"

Phil said, "I'll take stupid questions for five hundred, Alex," and loosened his shoulder as if getting ready for a punch.

"Because if you do, you'll get her to talk to me. You were the one who convinced her not to see me, and now you've got to convince her that she *has* to see me."

Phil looked around the parking lot, as if calling for somebody to witness this insanity.

James spoke slowly and clearly, enunciating each word. "There is something I can do to help her."

"Because you're Don Juan, right? You're gonna heal her with your love." The words were flippant, but Phil's voice was shaky with sheer hatred. Not just hatred for James, but for a universe that would give Poppy cancer.

"No. You've got it completely wrong. Look, you think

I was making out with her, or trifling with her affections or whatever. That's not what was going on at all. I let you think that because I was tired of getting the third degree from you— and because I didn't want you to know what we *were* doing."

"Sure, sure," Phil said in a voice filled with equal measures of sarcasm and contempt. "So what *were* you doing? Drugs?"

"This."

James had learned something from his first encounter with Poppy in the hospital. Show and tell should be done in that order. This time he didn't say anything; he just grabbed Phil by the hair and jerked his head back.

There was only a single light behind the store, but it was enough to give Phil a good view of the bared fangs looming over him. And it was more than enough for James, with his night vision, to see Phillip's green eyes dilate as he stared.

Phillip yelled, then went limp.

Not with fear, James knew. He wasn't a coward. With the shock of disbelief turning to belief.

Phillip swore. "You're a . . ."

"Right." James let him go.

Phil almost lost his balance. He grabbed at the Dumpster for support. "I don't believe it."

"Yes, you do," James said. He hadn't retracted his fangs, and he knew that his eyes were shining silver. Phil *had* to believe it with James standing right in front of him.

Phil apparently had the same idea. He was staring at James

as if he wanted to look away, but couldn't. The color had drained out of his face, and he kept swallowing as if he were going to be sick.

"God," he said finally. "I knew there was something wrong with you. Weird wrong. I could never figure out why you gave me the creeps. So this is it."

I disgust him, James realized. It's not just hatred anymore. He thinks I'm less than human.

It didn't augur well for the rest of James's plan.

"Now do you understand how I can help Poppy?"

Phil shook his head slowly. He was leaning against the wall, one hand still on the Dumpster.

James felt impatience rise in his chest. "Poppy has a disease. Vampires don't get diseases. Do you need a road map?"

Phillip's expression said he did.

"If," James said through his teeth, "I exchange enough blood with Poppy to turn her into a vampire, she won't have cancer anymore. Every cell in her body will change and she'll end up a perfect specimen: flawless, disease-free. She'll have powers that humans don't even dream of. And, incidentally, she'll be immortal."

There was a long, long silence as James watched this sink in with Phillip. Phil's thoughts were too jumbled and kaleidoscopic for James to make anything of them, but Phil's eyes got wider and his face more ashen.

At last Phil said, "You can't do that to her."

It was the *way* he said it. Not as if he were protesting an idea because it was too radical, too new. Not the knee-jerk overreaction that Poppy had had.

He said it with absolute conviction and utmost horror. As if James were threatening to steal Poppy's soul.

"It's the only way to save her *life*," James said.

Phil shook his head slowly again, eyes huge and trancelike. "No. No. She wouldn't want it. Not at that cost."

"What cost?" James was more than impatient now, he was defensive and exasperated. If he'd realized that this was going to turn into a philosophical debate, he would have picked somewhere less public. As it was, he had to keep all his senses on the alert for possible intruders.

Phil let go of the Dumpster and stood on his own two feet. There was fear mixed with the horror in his eyes, but he faced James squarely.

"It's just—there are some things that humans think are more important than just staying alive," he said. "You'll find that out."

I don't believe this, James thought. He sounds like a junior space captain talking to the alien invaders in a B movie. *You won't find Earth people quite the easy mark you imagine.*

Aloud, he said, "Are you nuts? Look, Phil, I was born in San Francisco. I'm not some bug-eyed monster from Alpha Centauri. I eat Wheaties for breakfast."

"And what do you eat for a midnight snack?" Phil asked, his green eyes somber and almost childlike. "Or are the fangs just for decoration?"

Walked right into that one, James's brain told him.

He looked away. "Okay. Touché. There are some differences. I never said I was a human. But I'm not some kind of—"

"If you're not a monster, then I don't know what is."

Don't kill him, James counseled himself frantically. You have to *convince* him. "Phil, we're not like what you see at the movies. We're not all-powerful. We can't dematerialize through walls or travel through time, and we don't need to kill to feed. We're not evil, at least not all of us. We're not damned."

"You're unnatural," Phillip said softly, and James could feel that he meant it from his heart. "You're *wrong.* You shouldn't exist."

"Because we're higher up on the food chain than you?"

"Because people weren't meant to . . . feed . . . on other people."

James didn't say that his people didn't think of Phillip's people as people. He said, "We only do what we have to do to survive. And Poppy's already agreed."

Phillip froze. "No. She wouldn't want to become like you."

"She wants to stay alive—or at least, she did, before she got mad at me. Now she's just irrational because she hasn't got enough of my blood in her to finish changing her. Thanks to you." He paused, then said deliberately, "Have you ever seen a three-week-old corpse, Phil? Because *that's* what she's going to become if I don't get to her."

Phil's face twisted. He whirled around and slammed a fist into the metal side of the Dumpster. "*Don't you think I know that?* I've been living with that since Monday night."

James stood still, heart pounding. Feeling the anguish Phil was giving off and the pain of Phil's injured hand. It was several seconds before he was able to say calmly, "And you think that's better than what I can give her?"

"It's lousy. It stinks. But, yes, it's better than turning into something that hunts people. That *uses* people. That's why all the girlfriends, isn't it?"

Once again, James couldn't answer right away. Phil's problem, he was realizing, was that Phil was far too smart for his own good. He thought too much. "Yeah. That's why all the girlfriends," he said at last, tiredly. Trying not to see this from Phil's point of view.

"Just tell me one thing, Rasmussen." Phillip straightened and looked him dead in the eye. "Did you"—he stopped and swallowed—"feed on Poppy—before she got sick?"

"No."

Phil let out his breath. "That's good. Because if you *had*, I'd have killed you."

James believed him. He was much stronger than Phil, much faster, and he'd never been afraid of a human before. But

just at that moment he had no doubt that Phil would somehow have found a way to do it.

"Look, there's something you don't understand," he said.
"Poppy *did* want this, and it's something we've already started.
She's only just beginning to change; if she dies now, she won't
become a vampire. But she might not die all the way, either.
She could end up a walking corpse. A zombie, you know?
Mindless. Body rotting, but immortal."

Phil's mouth quivered with revulsion. "You're just saying
that to scare me."

James looked away. "I've seen it happen."

"I don't believe you."

"I've seen it *firsthand*!" Dimly James realized he was yelling and that he'd grabbed Phil by the shirtfront. He was out of
control—and he didn't care. "I've seen it happen to somebody
I *cared* about, all right?"

And then, because Phil was still shaking his head: "I was
only four years old and I had a nanny. All the rich kids in San
Francisco have nannies. She was human."

"Let go," Phil muttered, pulling at James's wrist. He was
breathing hard—he didn't want to hear this.

"I was crazy about her. She gave me everything my mom
didn't. Love, attention—she was never too busy. I called her
Miss Emma."

"Let go."

"But my parents thought I was too attached to her. So they

took me on a little vacation—and they didn't let me feed. Not for three days. By the time they brought me back, I was starving. Then they sent Miss Emma up to put me to bed."

Phil had stopped fighting now. He stood with his head bowed and turned to one side so he wouldn't have to look at James. James threw his words at the averted face.

"I was only four. I couldn't stop myself. And the thing is, I wanted to. If you'd asked me who I'd rather have die, me or Miss Emma, I'd've said me. But when you're starving, you lose control. So I fed on her, and all the time I was crying and trying to stop. And when I finally could stop, I knew it was too late."

There was a pause. James suddenly realized that his fingers were locked in an agonizing cramp. He let go of Phil's shirt slowly. Phil said nothing.

"She was just lying there on the floor. I thought, wait, if I give her my own blood she'll be a vampire, and everything will be okay." He wasn't yelling anymore. He wasn't even really speaking to Phillip, but staring out into the dark parking lot. "So I cut myself and let the blood run into her mouth. She swallowed some of it before my parents came up and stopped me. But not enough."

A longer pause—and James remembered why he was telling the story. He looked at Phillip.

"She died that night—but not all the way. The two different kinds of blood were fighting inside her. So by morning she was walking around again—but she wasn't Miss Emma any-more. She drooled and her skin was gray and her eyes were flat like a corpse's. And when she started to—rot—my dad took her out to Inverness and buried her. He killed her first." Bile rose in James's throat and he added almost in a whisper, "I hope he killed her first."

Phil slowly turned around to look at him. For the first time that evening, there was something other than horror and fear in his face. Something like pity, James thought.

James took a deep breath. After thirteen years of silence he'd finally told the story—to Phillip North, of all people. But it was no good wondering about the absurdity. He had a point to drive home.

"So take my advice. If you don't convince Poppy to see me, make sure they don't do an autopsy on her. You don't want her walking around without her internal organs. And have a wooden stake ready for the time when you can't stand to look at her anymore."

The pity was gone from Phil's eyes. His mouth was a hard, trembling line.

"We won't let her turn into . . . some kind of half-alive abomination," he said. "Or a vampire, either. I'm sorry about what happened to your Miss Emma, but it doesn't change anything."

"*Poppy* should be the one to decide—"

But Phillip had reached his limit, and now he was simply

shaking his head. "Just keep away from my sister," he said. "That's all I want. If you do, I'll leave you alone. And if you don't—"

"What?"

"I'm going to tell everybody in El Camino what you are. I'm going to call the police and the mayor and I'm going to stand in the middle of the street and yell it."

James felt his hands go icy cold. What Phil didn't realize was that he'd just made it James's duty to kill him. It wasn't just that any human who stumbled on Night World secrets had to die, but that one actively threatening to *tell* about the Night World had to die immediately, no questions asked, no mercy given.

Suddenly James was so tired he couldn't see straight.

"Get out of here, Phil," he said in a voice drained of emotion and vitality both. "Now. And if you really want to protect Poppy, you won't tell anybody anything. Because they'll trace it back and find out that Poppy knows the secrets, too. And then they'll kill her—after bringing her in for questioning. It won't be fun."

"Who're 'they'? Your parents?"

"The Night People. We're all around you, Phil. Anybody you know could be one—including the mayor. So keep your mouth shut."

Phillip looked at him through narrowed eyes. Then he turned and walked to the front of the store.

James couldn't remember when he'd felt so empty. Everything he'd done had turned out wrong. Poppy was now in more kinds of danger than he could count.

And Phillip North thought he was unnatural and evil. What Phil didn't know was that most of the time James thought the same thing.

Phillip got halfway home before he remembered that he'd dropped the bag with Poppy's cranberry juice and wild cherry Popsicles. Poppy had hardly eaten in the last two days, and when she did get hungry, it was for something weird.

No—something *red*, he realized as he paid for a second time at the 7-Eleven. He felt a sick lurch in his stomach. Everything she wanted lately was red and at least semiliquid.

Did Poppy realize that herself?

He studied her when he went into her bedroom to give her a Popsicle. Poppy spent most of the time in bed now.

And she was so pale and still. Her green eyes were the only alive thing about her. They dominated her face, glittering with an almost savage awareness.

Cliff and Phil's mother were talking about getting round-the-clock nurses to be with her.

"Don't like the Popsicle?" Phil asked, dragging a chair to sit beside her bed.

Poppy was eyeing the thing with distaste. She took a tiny lick and grimaced.

Phillip watched her.

Another lick. Then she put the Popsicle into an empty plastic cup on her nightstand. "I don't know . . . I just don't feel hungry," she said, leaning back against the pillows. "Sorry you had to go out for nothing."

"No problem." God, she looks sick, Phil thought. "Is there anything else I can do for you?"

Eyes shut. Poppy shook her head. A very small motion. "You're a good brother," she said distantly.

She used to be so alive, Phil thought. Dad called her Kilowatt or Eveready. She used to *radiate* energy.

Without in the least meaning to, he found himself saying, "I saw James Rasmussen today."

Poppy stiffened. Her hands on the bedspread formed not fists, but claws. "He'd better keep away from here!"

There was something subtly wrong about her reaction. Something not-Poppy. Poppy could get fierce, sure, but Phil had never heard that animal tone in her voice before.

A picture flashed through Phil's mind. A creature from *Night of the Living Dead*, walking even though its intestines were spilling out. A living corpse like James's Miss Emma.

Was that really what would happen if Poppy died right now? Was she that much changed already?

"I'll scratch his eyes out if he comes around here," Poppy said, her fingers working on the spread like a cat kneading.

"Poppy—he told me the truth about what he really is."

Strangely, Poppy had no reaction. "He's scum," she said. "He's a reptile."

Something about her voice made Phillip's flesh creep. "And I told him you would never want to become something like that."

"I wouldn't," Poppy said shortly. "Not if it meant hanging around with *him* for eternity. I don't want to see him ever again."

Phil stared at her for a long moment. Then he leaned back and shut his eyes, one thumb jammed against his temple where the ache was worst.

Not just subtly wrong. He didn't want to believe it, but Poppy was *strange*. Irrational. And now that he thought about it, she'd been getting stranger every hour since James had been thrown out.

So maybe she *was* in some eerie in-between state. Not a human and not a vampire. And not able to think clearly. Just as James had said.

Poppy should be the one to decide.

There was something he had to ask her.

"Poppy?" He waited until she looked at him, her green eyes large and unblinking. "When we talked, James said that you'd agreed to let him—change you. Before you got mad at him. Is that right?"

Poppy's eyebrows lifted. "I'm mad at him," she confirmed, as if this was the only part of the question she'd processed.

"And you know why I like you? Because you've always hated him. Now we both hate him."

Phil thought for a moment, then spoke carefully. "Okay. But when you *weren't* mad at him, back then, did you want to turn into—what he is?"

Suddenly a gleam of rationality showed in Poppy's eyes. "I just didn't want to *die*," she said. "I was so scared—and I wanted to live. If the doctors could do anything for me, I'd try that. But they can't." She was sitting up now, staring into space as if she saw something terrible there. "You don't know what it feels like to know you're going to die," she whispered.

Waves of chills washed over Phillip. No, he didn't know that, but he did know—he could suddenly picture vividly— what it was going to be like for *him* after Poppy died. How empty the world was going to be without her.

For a long time they both sat in silence.

Then Poppy fell back onto the pillows again. Phillip could see pastel blue smudges under her eyes, as if the conversation had exhausted her. "I don't think it matters," she said in a faint but frighteningly cheerful voice. "I'm not going to die anyway. Doctors don't know everything."

So that's how she's dealing with it, Phillip thought. Total denial.

He had all the information he needed, though. He had a clear view of the situation. And he knew what he had to do now.

"I'll leave so you can get some rest," he said to Poppy, and patted her hand. It felt very cool and fragile, full of tiny bones like a bird's wing. "See you later."

He slipped out of the house without telling anyone where he was going. Once on the road, he drove very fast. It only took ten minutes to reach the apartment building.

He'd never been to James's apartment before.

James answered the door with a cold, "What are you doing here?"

"Can I come in? I've got something to say."

James stood back expressionlessly to let him in.

The place was roomy and bare. There was a single chair beside a very cluttered table, an equally cluttered desk, and a square unbeautiful couch. Cardboard boxes full of books and CDs were stacked in the corners. A door led to a spartan bedroom.

"What do you want?"

"First of all, I have to explain something. I know you can't help being what you are—but I can't help how I feel about it, either. You can't change, and neither can I. I need you to understand that from the beginning."

James crossed his arms over his chest, wary and defiant. "You can skip the lecture."

"I just need to make sure you understand, okay?"

"What do you *want*, Phil?"

Phil swallowed. It took two or three tries before he could get the words out past the blockage of his pride.

"I want you to help my sister."

CHAPTER 9

Poppy shifted on her bed.

She was unhappy. It was a hot, restless unhappiness that seemed to swarm underneath her skin. Coming from her body instead of from her mind. If she hadn't been so weak, she would have gotten up and tried to run the feeling off. But she had spaghetti for muscles now and she wasn't running anywhere.

Her mind was simply cloudy. She didn't try to think much anymore. She was happiest when she was asleep.

But tonight she couldn't sleep. She could still taste the wild cherry Popsicle in the corners of her mouth. She would have tried to wash the taste away, but the thought of water made her feel vaguely nauseated. Water's no good. Not what I need.

Poppy turned over and pressed her face into the pillow. She didn't know what she needed, but she knew she wasn't getting it.

A soft sound came from the hallway. Footsteps. The footsteps of at least two people. It didn't sound like her mother and Cliff, and anyway they'd gone to bed.

There was the lightest of knocks at her door, then a fan of light opened on the floor as the door cracked. Phil whispered, "Poppy, you asleep? Can I come in?"

To Poppy's slowly rising indignation, he *was* coming in, without waiting for an answer. And someone was with him.

Not just someone. *The* one. The one who had hurt Poppy worst of all. The betrayer. James.

Anger gave Poppy the strength to sit up. "Go away! I'll hurt you!" The most primitive and basic of warning-off messages. An animal reaction.

"Poppy, please let me talk to you," James said. And then something amazing happened. Even Poppy, in her befuddled state, recognized that it was amazing.

Phil said, "Please do it, Poppy. Just listen to him."

Phil siding with James?

Poppy was too confused to protest as James came and knelt by her bedside.

"Poppy, I know you're upset. And it's my fault; I made a mistake. I didn't want Phil to know what was really going on, and I told him I was just pretending to care for you. But it wasn't true."

Poppy frowned.

"If you search your feelings, you'll *know* it's not true. You're turning into a telepath, and I think you already have enough power to read me."

Behind James, Phil stirred as if uneasy at the mention of telepathy. "*I* can tell you it's not true," he said, causing both Poppy and James to look at him in surprise. "That's one thing I found out from talking to you," he added, speaking to James without looking at him. "You may be some kind of monster, but you really do care about Poppy. You're not trying to hurt her."

"*Now* you finally get it? After causing all this—?" James broke off and shook his head, turning back to Poppy. "Poppy, concentrate. Feel what I'm feeling. Find the truth for yourself."

I won't and you can't make me, Poppy thought. But the part of her that wanted to find out the truth was stronger than the irrational, angry part. Tentatively she *reached* for James— not with her hand, but with her mind. She couldn't have described to anyone how she did it. She just did it.

And she found James's mind, diamond-bright and burning with intensity. It wasn't the same as being one with him, the way she had been when they shared blood. It was like looking at him from the outside, sensing his emotions from a distance. But it was enough. The warmth and longing and protectiveness he had for her were all clear. So was the anguish: the pain he felt to know that she was hurting—and that she hated him.

Poppy's eyes filled. "You really do care," she whispered.

James's gray eyes met hers, and there was a look in them Poppy couldn't remember seeing before. "There are two cardinal rules in the Night World," he said steadily. "One is not to tell humans that it exists. The other is not to fall in love with a human. I've broken both of them."

Poppy was aware, vaguely, that Phillip was walking out of the room. The fan of light contracted as he half-shut the door behind him. James's face was partly in shadow.

"I could never tell you how I felt about you," James said. "I couldn't even admit it to myself. Because it puts you in terrible danger. You can't imagine what kind of danger."

"And you, too," Poppy said. It was the first time she'd really thought about this. Now the idea emerged from her muddled consciousness like a bubble in a pot of stew. "I mean," she said slowly, puzzling it out, "if it's against the rules to tell a human or love a human, and you break the rules, then there must be some punishment for *you*. . . ." Even as she said it, she sensed what the punishment was.

More of James's face went into shadow. "Don't you worry about that," he said in his old voice, his cool-guy voice.

Poppy never took advice, not even from James. A surge of irritation and anger swept through her—an animal surge, like the feverish restlessness. She could feel her eyes narrow and her fingers claw.

"Don't you tell me what to worry about!"

He frowned. "Don't you tell me not to tell you—" he

began, and then broke off. "What am I doing? You're still sick with the change and I'm just sitting here." He rolled up a sleeve of his windbreaker and drew a fingernail along his wrist. Where the nail cut, blood welled up.

It looked black in the darkness. But Poppy found her eyes fixing on its liquid beading in fascination. Her lips parted and her breath came faster.

"Come on," James said, and held his wrist in front of her. The next second Poppy had pounced and fixed her mouth on it as if she were trying to save him from a snakebite.

It was so natural, so easy. *This* is what she'd needed when she was dispatching Phil to get Popsicles and cranberry juice. This sweet, heady stuff was the real thing and nothing else was like it. Poppy sucked avidly.

It was all good: the closeness, the rich, dark-red taste; the strength and vitality that flooded through her, warming her to her fingertips. But best, better than any mere sensation, was the touch of James's mind. It made her giddy with pleasure.

How could she ever have mistrusted him? It seemed ridiculous now that she could *feel*, directly, how he felt about her. She would never know anyone the way she knew James.

I'm sorry, she thought to him, and felt her thought accepted, forgiven, cherished. Held gently by the cradling of James's mind.

It wasn't your fault, he told her.

Poppy's mind seemed to be clearing with every second that

went by. It was like waking up out of a deep and uncomfortable sleep. *I don't ever want this to end,* she thought, not really directing it at James, just thinking it.

But she felt a reaction in him—and then felt him bury the reaction quickly. Not quickly enough. Poppy had sensed it.

Vampires don't do this to each other.

Poppy was shocked. They would never have this glory again after she changed? She wouldn't believe that; she refused. There must be a way. . . .

Again, she felt the beginning of a reaction in James, but just as she was chasing it, he gently pulled his wrist back. "You'd better not take any more tonight," he said, and his real-world voice sounded strange to Poppy's ears. It wasn't as much *James* as his mental voice, and now she couldn't really feel him properly. They were two separate beings. The isolation was awful.

How could she survive if she could never touch his mind again? If she had to use *words*, which suddenly seemed as clumsy as smoke signals for communication? If she could never feel him fully, his whole being open to her?

It was cruel and unfair and all vampires must be idiots if they settled for anything less.

Before she could open her mouth to begin the clumsy process of verbally explaining this to James, the door moved. Phillip looked around it.

"Come on in," James said. "We've got a lot to talk about."

Phil was staring at Poppy. "Are you . . ." He stopped and

swallowed before finishing in a husky whisper. "Better?"

It didn't take telepathy to sense his disgust. He glanced at her mouth, and then quickly away. Poppy realized what he must be seeing. A stain as if she'd been eating berries. She rubbed at her lips with the back of her hand.

What she wanted to say was, it isn't disgusting. It's part of Nature. It's a way of giving life, pure life. It's secret and beautiful. It's *all right*.

What she said was, "Don't knock it till you've tried it."

Phillip's face convulsed in horror. And the weird thing was that on this subject James was in perfect agreement with him. Poppy could sense it—James thought sharing blood was dark and evil, too. He was filled with guilt. Poppy heaved a long, exasperated sigh, and added, *"Boys."*

"You're better," Phil said, cracking a faint smile.

"I guess I was pretty bizarre before," Poppy said. "Sorry."

"*Pretty* is not the word."

"It wasn't her fault," James said shortly to Phil. "She was dying—and hallucinating, sort of. Not enough blood to the brain."

Poppy shook her head. "I don't get it. You didn't take that much blood from me the last time. How could I not have enough blood to the brain?"

"It's not that," James said. "The two kinds of blood react against each other—they fight each other. Look, if you want a scientific explanation, it's something like this. Vampire blood destroys the hemoglobin—the red cells—in human blood. Once it destroys enough of the red cells, you stop getting the oxygen you need to think straight. And when it destroys more, you don't have the oxygen you need to live."

"So vampire blood is like poison," Phil said, in the tones of someone who knew it all along.

James shrugged. He wasn't looking at either Poppy or Phil. "In some ways. But in other ways it's like a universal cure. It makes wounds heal fast, makes flesh regenerate. Vampires can live on very little oxygen because their cells are so resilient. Vampire blood does everything—except carry oxygen."

A light went on in Poppy's brain. Dawning revelation— the mystery of Count Dracula explained. "Wait a minute," she said. "Is *that* why you need human blood?"

"That's one of the reasons," James said. "There are some . . . some more mystical things human blood does for us, but keeping us alive is the most basic one. We take a little and that carries oxygen through our system until our own blood destroys it. Then we take a little more."

Poppy settled back. "So that's it. And it *is* natural. . . ."

"Nothing about this is natural," Phil said, his disgust surfacing again.

"Yes, it is; it's like whatdoyoucallit, from biology class. Symbiosis—"

"It doesn't *matter* what it's like," James said. "We can't sit here and talk about it. We've got to make plans."

There was an abrupt silence as Poppy realized what kind of plans he was talking about. She could tell Phil was realizing it, too.

"You're not out of danger yet," James said softly, his eyes holding Poppy's. "It's going to take one more exchange of blood, and you should have it as soon as possible. Otherwise, you might relapse again. But we're going to have to plan the next exchange carefully."

"Why?" Phil said, at his most deliberately obstructive.

"Because it's going to kill me," Poppy said flatly before James could answer. And when Phil flinched, she went on ruthlessly, "That's what this is all *about*, Phil. It's not some little game James and I are playing. We have to deal with the reality, and the reality is that one way or another I'm going to die soon. And I'd rather die and wake up a vampire than die and not wake up at all."

There was another silence, during which James put his hand on hers. It was only then that Poppy realized she was shaking.

Phil looked up. Poppy could see that his face was drawn, his eyes dark. "We're twins. So how'd you get so much older than me?" he said in a muted voice.

A little hush, and then James said, "I think tomorrow night would be a good time to do it. It's Friday—do you think you can get your mom and Cliff out of the house for the night?"

Phil blinked. "I guess—if Poppy seems better, they might go out for a little while. If I said I'd stay with her."

"Convince them they need a break. I don't want them around."

"Can't you just make them not notice anything? Like you did with that nurse at the hospital?" Poppy asked.

"Not if I'm going to be concentrating on *you*," James said. "And there are certain people who can't be influenced by mind control at all—your brother, here, is one of them. Your mom could be another."

"All right; I'll get them to go out," Phillip said. He gulped, obviously uncomfortable and trying to hide it. "And once they're gone . . . then what?"

James looked at him inscrutably. "Then Poppy and I do what we have to do. And then *you* and I watch TV."

"Watch TV," Phil repeated, sounding numb.

"I've got to be here when the doctor comes—and the people from the funeral home."

Phil looked utterly horrified at the mention of the funeral home. For that matter, Poppy didn't feel too cheerful about it herself. If it weren't for the rich, strange blood coursing inside her, calming her . . .

"*Why?*" Phillip was demanding of James.

James shook his head, very slightly. His face was expressionless. "I just do," he said. "You'll understand later. For now, just trust me."

Poppy decided not to pursue it.

"So you guys are going to have to make up tomorrow," she

said. "In front of Mom and Cliff. Otherwise it'll be too weird for you to hang out together."

"It'll be too weird no matter what," Phil said under his breath. "All right. Come over tomorrow afternoon and we'll make up. And I'll get them to leave us with Poppy."

James nodded. "I'd better go now." He stood. Phil stepped back to let him out the door, but James hesitated by Poppy.

"You gonna be all right?" he asked in a low voice.

Poppy nodded staunchly.

"Tomorrow, then." He touched her cheek with his fingertips. The briefest contact, but it made Poppy's heart leap and it turned her words into the truth. She *would* be all right.

They looked at each other a moment, then James turned away.

Tomorrow, Poppy thought, watching the door close behind him. Tomorrow is the day I die.

One thing about it, Poppy thought—not many people were privileged to *know* exactly when they were going to die. So not many people had the chance to say goodbye the way she planned to.

It didn't matter that she wasn't *really* dying. When a caterpillar changes into a butterfly it loses its caterpillar life. No more shinnying up twigs, no more eating leaves.

No more El Camino High School, Poppy thought. No more sleeping in this bed.

She was going to have to leave it all behind. Her family, her hometown. Her entire human life. She was starting out into a strange new future with no idea of what was ahead. All she could do was trust James—and trust her own ability to adapt.

It was like looking at a pale and curving road stretching in front of her, and not being able to see where it went as it disappeared into the darkness.

No more Rollerblading down the boardwalk at Venice Beach, Poppy thought. No more slap of wet feet on concrete at the Tamashaw public pool. No more shopping at the Village.

To say goodbye, she looked at every corner of her room. Goodbye white-painted dresser. Goodbye desk where she had sat writing hundreds of letters—as proven by the stains where she'd dropped sealing wax on the wood. Goodbye bed, goodbye misty white bed curtains that had made her feel like an Arabian princess in a fairy tale. Goodbye stereo.

Ouch, she thought. My stereo. And my *CDs.* I can't leave them; I can't. . . .

But of course she could. She would have to.

It was probably just as well that she had to deal with the stereo before she walked out of her room. It built her up to start dealing with the loss of *people.*

"Hi, Mom," she said shakily, in the kitchen.

"Poppy! I didn't know you were up."

She hugged her mother hard, in that one moment aware of so many little sensations: the kitchen tile under her bare feet, the faint coconut smell that clung to her mother's hair from her shampoo. Her mother's arms around her, and the warmth of her mother's body.

"Are you hungry, sweetie? You look so much better."

Poppy couldn't stand to look into her mother's anxiously hopeful face, and the thought of food made her nauseated. She burrowed back into her mother's shoulder.

"Just hold me a minute," she said.

It came to her, then, that she wasn't going to be able to say goodbye to everything after all. She couldn't tie up all the loose ends of her life in one afternoon. She might be privileged to know that this was her last day here, but she was going out just like everyone else—unprepared.

"Just remember I love you," she muttered into her mother's shoulder, blinking back tears.

She let her mother put her back to bed, then. She spent the rest of the day making phone calls. Trying to learn a *little* bit about the life she was about to exit, the people she was supposed to know. Trying to appreciate it all, *fast*, before she had to leave it.

"So, Elaine, I miss you," she said into the mouthpiece, her eyes fixed on the sunlight coming in her window.

"So, Brady, how's it going?"

"So, Laura, thanks for the flowers."

"Poppy, are you *okay*?" they all said. "When are we going to see you again?"

Poppy couldn't answer. She wished she could call her dad, but nobody knew where he was.

She also wished she had actually *read* the play *Our Town* when she'd been assigned it last year, instead of using Cliffs-Notes and quick thinking to fake it. All she could remember now was that it was about a dead girl who got the chance to look at one ordinary day in her life and really appreciate it. It might have helped her sort out her own feelings now—but it was too late.

I wasted a lot of high school, Poppy realized. I used my brains to outsmart the teachers—and that really wasn't very smart at all.

She discovered in herself a new respect for Phil, who actually used his brain to learn things. Maybe her brother wasn't just a pitiful straitlaced grind after all. Maybe—oh, God—*he'd* been right all along.

I'm changing so much, Poppy thought, and she shivered.

Whether it was the strange alien blood in her or the cancer itself or just part of growing up, she didn't know. But she was changing.

The doorbell rang. Poppy knew who it was without leaving the room. She could sense James.

He's here to start the play, Poppy thought, and looked at her clock. Incredible. It was almost four o'clock already.

Time literally seemed to be flying by.

Don't panic. You have hours yet, she told herself, and

picked up the phone again. But it seemed only minutes later that her mother came knocking on the bedroom door.

"Sweetie, Phil thinks we should go out—and James has come over—but I told him I don't think you want to see him—and I don't really want to leave you at night. . . ." Her mother was uncharacteristically flustered.

"No, I'm happy to see James. Really. And I think you *should* take a break. Really."

"Well—I'm glad you and James have made up. But I still don't know. . . ."

It took time to convince her, to persuade her that Poppy was so much better, that Poppy had weeks or months ahead of her to live. That there was no reason to stick around on this particular Friday night.

But at last Poppy's mother kissed her and agreed. And then there was nothing to do but say goodbye to Cliff. Poppy got a hug from him and finally forgave him for not being her dad.

You did your best, she thought as she disengaged from his crisp dark suit and looked at his boyishly square jaw. And you're going to be the one to take care of Mom—afterward. So I forgive you. You're all right, really.

And then Cliff and her mom were walking out, and it was the last time, the very last time to say goodbye. Poppy called it after them and they both turned and smiled.

When they were gone, James and Phil came into Poppy's room. Poppy looked at James. His gray eyes were opaque, revealing nothing of his feelings.

"Now?" she said, and her voice trembled slightly.

"Now."

CHAPTER 10

"Things have to be right," Poppy said. "Things have to be just right for this. Get some candles, Phil."

Phil was looking ashen and haggard. "Candles?"

"As many as you can find. And some pillows. I need lots of pillows." She knelt by the stereo to examine a haphazard pile of CDs. Phil stared at her briefly, then went out.

"*Structures from Silence* . . . no. Too repetitious," Poppy said, rummaging through the pile. "*Deep Forest*—no. Too hyper. I need something *ambient.*"

"How about this?" James picked a CD up. Poppy looked at the label.

Music to Disappear In.

Of course. It was perfect. Poppy took the CD and met James's gaze. Usually he referred to the haunting soft strains of ambient music as "New Age mush."

"You understand," she said quietly.

"Yes. But you're not dying, Poppy. This isn't a death scene you're setting up."

"But I'm going away. I'm changing." Poppy couldn't explain exactly, but something in her said she was doing the right thing. She was dying to her old life. It was a solemn occasion, a Passage.

And of course, although neither of them mentioned it, they both knew she *might* die for good. James had been very frank about that—some people didn't make it through the transition.

Phil came back with candles, Christmas candles, emergency candles, scented votive candles. Poppy directed him to place them around the room and light them. She herself went to the bathroom to change into her best nightgown. It was flannel, with a pattern of little strawberries.

Just imagine, she thought as she left the bathroom. This is the last time I'll ever walk down this hall, the last time I'll push open my bedroom door.

The bedroom was beautiful. The soft glow of candlelight gave it an aura of sanctity, of mystery. The music was unearthly and sweet, and Poppy felt she could fall into it forever, the way she fell in her dreams.

Poppy opened the closet and used a hanger to bat a tawny stuffed lion and a floppy gray Eeyore down from the top shelf. She took them to her bed and put them beside the mounded pillows. Maybe it was stupid, maybe it was childish, but she wanted them with her.

She sat on the bed and looked at James and Phillip.

They were both looking at her. Phil was clearly upset, touching his mouth to stop its trembling. James was upset, too, although only someone who knew him as well as Poppy did would have been able to tell.

"It's all right," Poppy told them. "Don't you see? *I'm* all right, so there's no excuse for you not to be."

And the strange thing was, it was the truth. She was all right. She felt calm and clear now, as if everything had become very simple. She saw the road ahead of her, and all she had to do was follow it, step by step.

Phil came over to squeeze her hand. "How does this—how does this work?" he asked James huskily.

"First we'll exchange blood," James said—speaking to Poppy. Looking only at her. "It doesn't have to be a lot; you're right on the border of changing already. Then the two kinds of blood fight it out—sort of the last battle, if you see what I mean." He smiled faintly and painfully, and Poppy nodded.

"While that's happening you'll feel weaker and weaker. And then you'll just—go to sleep. The change happens while you're asleep."

"And when do I wake up?" Poppy asked.

"I'll give you a kind of posthypnotic suggestion about that. Tell you to wake up when I come to get you. Don't worry about it; I've got all the details figured out. All you need to do is rest."

Phil was running nervous hands through his hair, as if he was just now thinking about what kind of details he and James were going to have to deal with. "Wait a minute," he said in almost a croak. "When—when you say 'sleep'—she's going to look . . ."

"Dead," Poppy supplied, when his voice ran out.

James gave Phil a cold look. "Yes. We've been over this."

"And then—we're really going to—what's going to *happen* to her?"

James glared.

"It's okay," Poppy said softly. "Tell him."

"You know what's going to happen," James said through clenched teeth to Phillip. "She can't just disappear. We'd have the police *and* the Night People after us, looking for her. No, it's got to seem that she died from the cancer, and that means everything's got to happen exactly the way it would if she *had* died."

Phil's sick expression said he wasn't at his most rational. "You're sure there isn't any other way?"

"No," James said.

Phil wet his lips. "Oh, God."

Poppy herself didn't want to dwell on it too much. She said fiercely, "*Deal* with it, Phil. You've got to. And remember, if it doesn't happen now it's going to happen in a few weeks—for real."

Phil was holding on to one of the brass bedposts so hard

that his knuckles were pale. But he'd gotten the point, and there was no one better than Phil at bracing himself. "You're right," he said thinly, with the ghost of his old efficient manner. "Okay, I'm dealing with it."

"Then let's get started," Poppy said, making her voice calm and steady. As if she were dealing with everything effortlessly herself.

James said to Phil, "You don't want to see this part. Go out and watch TV for a few minutes."

Phil hesitated, then nodded and left.

"One thing," Poppy said to James as she scooted to the middle of the bed. She was still trying desperately to sound casual. "After the funeral—well, I'll be asleep, won't I? I won't wake up . . . you know. In my nice little coffin." She looked up at him. "It's just that I'm claustrophobic, a little."

"You won't wake up there," James said. "Poppy, I wouldn't let that happen to you. Trust me; I've thought of everything."

Poppy nodded. I do trust you, she thought.

Then she held her arms out to him.

He touched her neck, so she tilted her chin back. As the blood was drawn from her, she felt her mind drawn into his.

Don't worry, Poppy. Don't be afraid. All his thoughts were ferociously protective. And even though it only confirmed that there was something to be afraid *of,* that this could go wrong, Poppy felt peaceful. The direct sense of his love made her calm, flooded her with light.

She suddenly felt distance and height and depth—spaciousness. As if her horizons had expanded almost to infinity in an instant. As if she'd discovered a new dimension. As if there were no limits or obstacles to what she and James could do together.

She felt . . . free.

I'm getting light-headed, she realized. She could feel herself going limp in James's arms. Swooning like a wilting flower.

I've taken enough, James said in her mind. The warm animal mouth on her throat pulled back. "Now it's your turn."

This time, though, he didn't make the cut at his wrist. He took off his T-shirt and, with a quick, impulsive gesture, ran a fingernail along the base of his throat.

Oh, Poppy thought. Slowly, almost reverently, she leaned forward. James's hand supported the back of her head. Poppy put her arms around him, feeling his bare skin under the flannel of her nightgown.

It was better this way. But if James was right, it was another last time. She and James could never exchange blood again.

I can't accept that, Poppy thought, but she couldn't concentrate on anything for very long. This time, instead of clearing her brain, the wild, intoxicating vampire blood was making her more confused. More heavy and sleepy.

James?

It's all right. It's the beginning of the change.

Heavy . . . sleepy . . . warm. Lapped in salty ocean waves.

She could almost picture the vampire blood trickling through her veins, conquering everything in its path. It was ancient blood, primeval. It was changing her into something old, something that had been around since the dawn of time. Something primitive and basic.

Every molecule in her body, changing . . .

Poppy, can you hear me? James was shaking her slightly. Poppy had been so engrossed in the sensations that she hadn't even realized she wasn't drinking any longer. James was cradling her.

"Poppy."

It was an effort to open her eyes. "I'm all right. Just . . . sleepy."

His arms tightened around her, then he laid her gently on the mounded pillows. "You can rest now. I'll get Phil."

But before he went, he kissed her on the forehead.

My first kiss, Poppy thought, her eyes drifting shut again. And I'm comatose. Great.

She felt the bed give under weight and looked up to see Phil. Phil looked very nervous, sitting gingerly, staring at Poppy. "So what's happening now?" he asked.

"The vampire blood's taking over," James said.

Poppy said, "I'm really sleepy."

There was no pain. Just a feeling of wanting to glide away. Her body now felt warm and numb, as if she were insulated by a soft, thick aura.

"Phil? I forgot to say—thank you. For helping out. And everything. You're a good brother, Phil."

"You don't have to say that now," Phil said tersely. "You can say it later. I'm still going to be here later, you know."

But I might not be, Poppy thought. This is all a gamble. And I'd never take it, except that the only alternative was to give up without even trying to fight.

I fought, didn't I? At least I fought.

"Yes, you did," Phil said, his voice trembling. Poppy hadn't been aware she was speaking aloud. "You've always been a fighter," Phil said. "I've learned so much from you."

Which was funny, because she'd learned so much from *him*, even if most of it was in the last twenty-four hours. She wanted to tell him that, but there was so much to say, and she was so tired. Her tongue felt thick; her whole body weak and languorous.

"Just . . . hold my hand," she said, and she could hear that her voice was no louder than a breath. Phillip took one of her hands and James the other.

That was good. This was the way to do it, with Eeyore and her lion on the pillows beside her and Phil and James holding her hands, keeping her safe and anchored.

One of the candles was scented with vanilla, a warm and homey smell. A smell that reminded her of being a kid. Nilla wafers and naptime. That was what this was like. Just a nap in Miss Spurgeon's kindergarten, with the sun slanting across the floor and James on a mat beside her.

So safe, so serene . . .

"Oh, Poppy," Phil whispered.

James said, "You're doing great, kiddo. Everything's just right."

That was what Poppy needed to hear. She let herself fall backward into the music, and it *was* like falling in a dream, without fear. It was like being a raindrop falling into the ocean that had started you.

At the last moment she thought, I'm not ready. But she already knew the answer to that. Nobody was ever ready.

But she'd been stupid—she'd forgotten the most important thing. She'd never told James she loved him. Not even when he'd said he loved her.

She tried to get enough air, enough strength to say it. But it was too late. The outside world was gone and she couldn't feel her body any longer. She was floating in the darkness and the music, and all she could do now was sleep.

"Sleep," James said, leaning close to Poppy. "Don't wake up until I call you. Just sleep."

Every muscle in Phil's body was rigid. Poppy looked so peaceful—pale, with her hair spread out in coppery curls on the pillow, and her eyelashes black on her cheeks and her lips parted as she breathed gently. She looked like a porcelain baby doll. But the more peaceful she got, the more terrified Phil felt.

I can deal with this, he told himself. I *have* to.

Poppy gave a soft exhalation, and then suddenly she was moving. Her chest heaved once, twice. Her hand tightened on Phil's and her eyes flew open—but she didn't seem to be seeing anything. She simply looked astonished.

"Poppy!" Phil grabbed at her, getting a handful of flannel nightgown. She was so small and fragile inside it. "Poppy!"

The heaving gasps stopped. For one moment Poppy was suspended in air, then her eyes closed and she fell back on the pillows. Her hand was limp in Phil's.

Phil lost all rationality.

"Poppy," he said, hearing the dangerous, unbalanced tone in his own voice. "Poppy, come on. Poppy, wake up!"—on a rising note. His hands were shaking violently, scrabbling at Poppy's shoulders.

Other hands pushed his away. "What the hell are you doing?" James said quietly.

"Poppy? Poppy?" Phil kept staring at her. Her chest wasn't moving. Her face had a look of—innocent release. The kind of newness you only see in babies.

And it was—changing. Taking on a white, transparent look. It was uncanny, ghostlike, and even though Phil had never seen a corpse, he knew instinctively that this was the death pallor.

Poppy's essence had left her. Her body was flat and tone-less, no longer inflated by the vital spirit. Her hand in Phil's was slack, not like the hand of a sleeping person. Her skin had lost its shine, as if somebody had breathed on it softly.

Phil threw back his head and let out an animal sound. It wasn't human. It was a howl.

"You killed her!" He tumbled off the bed and lurched toward James. "You said she was just going to sleep, but you killed her! She's dead!"

James didn't back away from the attack. Instead, he grabbed Phil and dragged him out into the hallway.

"Hearing is the last sense to go," he snarled in Phillip's ear. "She may be able to *hear* you."

Phil wrenched free and ran toward the living room. He didn't know what he was doing, he only knew that he needed to destroy things. Poppy was dead. She was gone. He grabbed the couch and flipped it over, then kicked the coffee table over, too. He snatched up a lamp, yanked its cord out of the socket, and threw it toward the fireplace.

"Stop it!" James shouted over the crash. Phil saw him and ran at him. The sheer force of his charge knocked James backward into the wall. They fell to the floor together in a heap.

"You—killed her!" Phil gasped, trying to get his hands around James's throat.

Silver. James's eyes blazed like the molten metal. He grabbed Phil's wrists in a painful grip.

"Stop it *now*, Phillip," he hissed.

Something about the way he said it made Phil stop. Almost sobbing, he struggled to get air into his lungs.

"I'll kill *you* if I have to, to keep Poppy safe," James said, his voice still savage and menacing. "And she's only safe if you stop this and do exactly what I tell you to. *Exactly* what I tell you. Understand?" He shook Phil hard, nearly banging Phil's head into the wall.

Strangely enough, it was the right thing to say. James was saying he cared about Poppy. And weird as it might sound, Phil had come to trust James to tell the truth.

The raging red insanity in Phil's brain died away. He took a long breath.

"Okay. I understand," he said hoarsely. He was used to being in charge—both of himself and of other people. He didn't like James giving him orders. But in this case there was no help for it. "But—she is dead, isn't she?"

"It depends on your definition," James said, letting go and slowly pushing himself off the floor. He scanned the living room, his mouth grim. "Nothing went wrong, Phil. Everything went just the way it was supposed to—except for this. I was going to let your parents come back and find her, but we don't have that option now. There isn't any way to explain this mess, except the truth."

"The truth being?"

"That you went in there and found her dead and went berserk. And then I called your parents—you know what restaurant they're at, don't you?"

"It's Valentino's. My mom said they were lucky to get in."

"Okay. That'll work. But first we have to clean up the bedroom. Get all the candles and stuff out. It's got to look as if she just went to sleep, like any other night."

Phil glanced at the sliding glass door. It was just getting dark. But then Poppy had been sleeping a lot these last few days. "We'll say she got tired and told us to go watch TV," he said slowly, trying to conquer his dazed feeling and be clearheaded. "And then I went in after a while and checked on her."

"Right," James said, with a faint smile that didn't reach his eyes.

It didn't take long to clear out the bedroom. The hardest thing was that Phil had to keep looking at Poppy, and every time he looked, his heart lurched. She looked so tiny, so delicate-limbed. A Christmas angel in June.

He hated to take the stuffed animals away from her.

"She is going to wake up, isn't she?" he said, without looking at James.

"God, I hope so," James said, and his voice was very tired. It sounded more like a prayer than a wish. "If she doesn't you won't have to come after me with a stake, Phil. I'll take care of it myself."

Phil was shocked—and angry. "Don't be stupid," he said brutally. "If Poppy stood for anything—if she *stands* for anything—it's for life. Throwing your life away would be like a slap in her face. Besides, even if it goes wrong now, you did your best. Blaming yourself is just stupid."

James looked at him blankly, and Phil realized they'd managed to surprise each other. Then James nodded slowly. "Thanks."

It was a milestone, the first time they'd ever been on precisely the same wavelength. Phillip felt an odd connection between them.

He looked away and said briskly, "Is it time to call the restaurant?"

James glanced at his watch. "In just a few minutes."

"If we wait too long they're going to have left by the time we call."

"That doesn't matter. What matters is that we don't have any paramedics trying to resuscitate her, or taking her to the hospital. Which means she's got to be cold by the time anybody gets here."

Phil felt a wave of dizzy horror. "You're a cold-blooded snake after all."

"I'm just practical," James said wearily, as if speaking to a child. He touched one of Poppy's marble-white hands where it lay on the bedspread. "All right. It's time. I'm going to call. You can go berserk again if you want to."

Phil shook his head. He didn't have the energy anymore. But he did feel like crying, which was almost as good. Crying and crying like a kid who was lost and hurt.

"Get my mom," he said thickly.

He knelt on the floor beside Poppy's bed and waited.

Poppy's music was off and he could hear the TV in the family room. He had no sense of time passing until he also heard a car in the driveway.

Then he leaned his forehead against Poppy's mattress. His tears were absolutely genuine. At that moment he was sure he'd lost her forever.

"Brace yourself," James said from behind him. "They're here."

CHAPTER 11

The next few hours were the worst of Phil's life.

First and foremost was his mother. As soon as she walked in, Phil's priorities changed from wanting her to comfort him to wanting to comfort her. And of course there wasn't any comfort. All he could do was hold on to her.

It's too cruel, he thought dimly. There ought to be a way to tell her. But she would never believe it, and if she did, she'd be in danger, too. . . .

Eventually the paramedics did come, but only after Dr. Franklin had arrived.

"I called him," James said to Phil during one of the interludes when Phil's mom was crying on Cliff.

"Why?"

"To keep things simple. In this state, doctors can issue a death certificate if they've seen you within the last twenty days and they know the cause of death. We don't want any hospitals or coroners."

Phil shook his head. "Why? What's your problem with hospitals?"

"My problem," James said in a clipped, distinct voice, "is that in hospitals they do autopsies."

Phil froze. He opened his mouth but no sound came out.

"And in funeral homes they do embalming. Which is why I need to be around when they come to pick up the body. I need to influence their minds not to embalm her, or sew her lips shut, or—"

Phil bolted for the bathroom and was sick. He hated James again.

But nobody took Poppy to the hospital, and Dr. Franklin didn't mention an autopsy. He just held Phil's mother's hand and spoke quietly about how these things could happen suddenly, and how at least Poppy had been spared any pain.

"But she was so much better today," Phil's mother whispered through tears. "Oh, my baby, my baby. She'd been getting worse, but today she was *better*."

"It happens like that sometimes," Dr. Franklin said. "It's almost as if they rally for a last burst of life."

"But I wasn't *there* for her," Phil's mom said, and now there weren't any tears, just the terrible grating sound of guilt. "She was alone when she died."

Phil said, "She was asleep. She just went to sleep and

never woke up. If you look at her, you can see how peaceful it was."

He kept saying things like that, and so did Cliff and so did the doctor, and eventually the paramedics went away. And sometime after that, while his mother was sitting on Poppy's bed and stroking her hair, the people from the mortuary came.

"Just give me a few minutes," Phil's mother said, dry-eyed and pale. "I need a few minutes alone with her."

The mortuary men sat awkwardly in the family room, and James stared at them. Phil knew what was going on. James was fixing in their minds the fact that there was to be no embalming.

"Religious reasons, is that it?" one of the men said to Cliff, breaking a long silence.

Cliff stared at him, eyebrows coming together. "What are you talking about?"

The man nodded. "I understand. It's no problem."

Phil understood, too. Whatever the man was hearing, it wasn't what Cliff was saying.

"The only thing is, you'll want to have the viewing right away," the other man said to Cliff. "Or else a closed casket."

"Yes, it was unexpected," Cliff said, his face straightening out. "It's been a very short illness."

So now *he* wasn't hearing what the men were saying. Phil looked at James and saw sweat trickling down his face. Clearly it was a struggle to control three minds at once.

At last Cliff went in and got Phil's mother. He led her to the master bedroom to keep her from seeing what happened next.

What happened was that the two men went into Poppy's room with a body bag and a gurney. When they came out, there was a small, delicate hump in the bag.

Phil felt himself losing rationality again. He wanted to knock things down. He wanted to run a marathon to get away.

Instead, his knees started to buckle and his vision grayed out.

Hard arms held him up, led him to a chair. "Hang on," James said. "Just a few more minutes. It's almost over."

Right then Phil could almost forgive him for being a bloodsucking monster.

It was very late that night when everyone finally went to bed. To bed, not to sleep. Phil was one solid ache of misery from his throat down to his feet, and he lay awake with the light on until the sun came up.

The funeral home was like a Victorian mansion, and the room Poppy was in was filled with flowers and people. Poppy herself was in a white casket with gold fittings, and from far away she looked as if she were sleeping.

Phil didn't like to look at her. He looked instead at the visitors who kept coming in and filling the viewing room and the dozens of wooden pews. He'd never realized how many people loved Poppy.

"She was so full of life," her English teacher said.

"I can't believe she's gone," a guy from Phil's football team said.

"I'll never forget her," one of her friends said, crying.

Phil wore a dark suit and stood with his mother and Cliff. It was like a receiving line for a wedding. His mother kept saying, "Thank you for coming," and hugging people. The people went over and touched the casket gently and cried.

And in the process of greeting so many mourners, something strange happened. Phil got drawn in. The reality of Poppy's death was *so* real that all the vampire stuff began to seem like a dream. Bit by bit, he started to believe the story he was acting out.

After all, everybody else was so sure. Poppy had gotten cancer, and now she was dead. Vampires were just superstition.

James didn't come to the viewing.

Poppy was dreaming.

She was walking by the ocean with James. It was warm and she could smell salt and her feet were wet and sandy. She was wearing a new bathing suit, the kind that changes color when it gets wet. She hoped James would notice the suit, but he didn't say anything about it.

Then she realized he was wearing a mask. That was strange, because he was going to get a very weird tan with most of his face covered up.

"Shouldn't you take that off?" she said, thinking he might need help.

"I wear it for my health," James said—only it wasn't James's voice.

Poppy was shocked. She reached out and pulled the mask away.

It wasn't James. It was a boy with ash blond hair, even lighter than Phil's. Why hadn't she noticed his hair earlier? His eyes were green—and then they were blue.

"Who are you?" Poppy demanded. She was afraid.

"That would be telling." He smiled. His eyes were violet. Then he lifted his hand, and she saw that he was holding a poppy. At least, it was shaped like a poppy, but it was black. He caressed her cheek with the flower.

"Just remember," he said, still smiling whimsically. "Bad magic happens."

"What?"

"Bad magic happens," he said and turned and walked away. She found herself holding the poppy. He didn't leave any footprints in the sand.

Poppy was alone and the ocean was roaring. Clouds were gathering overhead. She wanted to wake up now, but she couldn't, and she was alone and scared. She dropped the flower as anguish surged through her.

"James!"

• • •

Phil sat up in bed, heart pounding.

God, what had that been? Something like a shout—in Poppy's voice.

I'm hallucinating.

Which wasn't surprising. It was Monday, the day of Poppy's funeral. In—Phil glanced at the clock—about four hours he had to be at the church. No wonder he was dreaming about her.

But she had sounded so scared. . . .

Phil put the thought out of his mind. It wasn't even hard. He'd convinced himself that Poppy was dead, and dead people didn't shout.

At the funeral, though, Phil got a shock. His father was there. He was even wearing something resembling a suit, although the jacket didn't match the trousers and his tie was askew.

"I came as soon as I heard. . . ."

"Well, where *were* you?" Phil's mother said, the fine lines of strain showing around her eyes, the way they always did when she had to deal with Phil's father.

"Backpacking in the Blue Ridge Mountains. Next time, I swear, I'll leave an address. I'll check my messages. . . ." He began to cry. Phil's mom didn't say anything else. She just reached for him, and Phil's heart twisted at the way they clung to each other.

He knew his dad was irresponsible and hopelessly behind

in child support and flaky and a failure. But nobody had ever loved Poppy more. Right then, Phil couldn't disapprove of him, not even with Cliff standing there for comparison.

The shock came when his dad turned to Phil before the service. "You know, she came to me last night," he said in a low voice. "Her spirit, I mean. She visited me."

Phil looked at him. This was the kind of weird statement that had brought on the divorce. His father had always talked about peculiar dreams and seeing things that weren't there. Not to mention collecting articles about astrology, numerology, and UFOs.

"I didn't see her, but I heard her calling. I just wish she hadn't sounded so frightened. Don't tell your mother, but I got the feeling she's not at rest." He put his hands over his face.

Phil felt every hair on the back of his neck stand up.

But the spooky feeling was drowned almost immediately in the sheer grief of the funeral. In hearing things like "Poppy will live on forever in our hearts and memories." A silver hearse led the way to Forest Park cemetery, and everyone stood in the June sunshine as the minister said some last words over Poppy's casket. By the time Phil had to put a rose on the casket, he was shaking.

It was a terrible time. Two of Poppy's girlfriends collapsed in near-hysterical sobs. Phillip's mother doubled over and had to be led away from the casket. There was no time to think— then or at the potluck at Phil's house afterward.

But it was at the house that Phil's two worlds collided. In the middle of all the milling confusion, he saw James.

He didn't know what to do. James didn't fit into what was going on here. Phil had half a mind to go over and tell him to get out, that the sick joke was over.

Before he could do anything, James walked up and said under his breath, "Be ready at eleven o'clock tonight."

Phil was jolted. "For what?"

"Just be ready, okay? And have some of Poppy's clothes with you. Whatever won't be missed." Phil didn't say anything, and James gave him an exasperated sideways look.

"We have to get her *out*, stupid. Or did you want to leave her there?"

Crash. That was the sound of worlds colliding. For a moment Phil was spinning in space with his feet on neither one.

Then with the normal world in shards around him, he leaned against a wall and whispered, "I can't. I can't do it. You're crazy."

"You're the one who's crazy. You're acting like it never happened. And you have to help, because I can't do it alone. She's going to be disoriented at first, like a sleepwalker. She'll *need* you."

That galvanized Phil. He jerked to stand up straight and whispered, "Did you hear her last night?"

James looked away. "She wasn't awake. She was just dreaming."

"How could we hear her from so far away? Even my *dad* heard it. Listen." He grabbed James by the lapel of his jacket. "Are you sure she's okay?"

"A minute ago you were convinced she was dead and gone. Now you want guarantees that she's fine. Well, I can't give you any." He stared Phil down with eyes as cold as gray ice. "I've never done this before, all right? I'm just going by the book. And there are always things that can go wrong. *But*," he said tersely when Phil opened his mouth, "the one thing I *do* know is that if we leave her where she is, she's going to have a very unpleasant awakening. Get it?"

Phil's hand unclenched slowly and he let go of the jacket. "Yeah. I'm sorry. I just can't believe any of this." He looked up to see that James's expression had softened slightly. "But if she was yelling last night, then she was alive then, right?"

"And strong," James said. "I've never known a stronger telepath. She's really going to be something."

Phil tried not to picture what. Of course, James was a vampire, and he looked perfectly normal—most of the time. But Phil's mind kept throwing out pictures of Poppy as a Hollywood monster. Red eyes, chalky skin, and dripping teeth.

If she came out like that, he'd try to love her. But part of him might want to get a stake.

Forest Park cemetery was completely different at night. The darkness seemed very thick. There was a sign on the iron gate that said, "No visitors after sunset," but the gate itself was open.

I don't want to be here, Phil thought.

James drove down the single lane road that curved around the cemetery and parked underneath a huge and ancient gingko tree.

"What if somebody sees us? Don't they have a guard or something?"

"They have a night watchman. He's asleep. I took care of it before I picked you up." James got out and began unloading an amazing amount of equipment from the backseat of the Integra.

Two heavy duty flashlights. A crowbar. Some old boards. A couple of tarps. And two brand-new shovels.

"Help me carry this stuff."

"What's it all *for*?" But Phil helped. Gravel crunched under his feet as he followed James on one of the little winding paths. They went up some weathered wooden stairs and down the other side and then they were in Toyland.

That was what somebody at the funeral had called it. Phil had overheard two business friends of Cliff's talking about it. It was a section of the cemetery where mostly kids were buried. You could tell without even looking at the headstones because there were teddy bears and things on the graves.

Poppy's grave was right on the edge of Toyland. It didn't have a headstone yet, of course. There was only a green plastic marker.

James dumped his armload on the grass and then knelt to examine the ground with a flashlight.

Phil stood silently, looking around the cemetery. He was still scared, partly with the normal fear that they'd get caught before they got finished, and partly with the supernatural fear that they *wouldn't*. The only sounds were crickets and distant traffic. Tree branches and bushes moved gently in the wind.

"Okay," James said. "First we've got to peel this sod off."

"Huh?" Phil hadn't even thought about why there was already grass on the new grave. But of course it was sod. James had found the edge of one strip and was rolling it up like a carpet.

Phil found another edge. The strips were about six feet long by one and a half feet wide. They were heavy, but it wasn't too hard to roll them up and off the foot of the grave.

"Leave 'em there. We've got to put them on again afterward," James grunted. "We don't want it to look as if this place has been disturbed."

A light went on for Phil. "*That's* why the tarps and stuff."

"Yeah. A little mess won't be suspicious. But if we leave dirt scattered everywhere, somebody's going to wonder." James laid the boards around the perimeter of the grave, then spread the tarps on either side. Phil helped him straighten them.

What was left where the sod had been was fresh, loamy soil. Phil positioned a flashlight and picked up a shovel.

I don't believe I'm doing this, he thought.

But he was doing it. And as long as all he thought about was the physical work, the job of digging a hole in the ground, he was okay. He concentrated on that and stepped on the shovel.

It went straight into the dirt, with no resistance. It was easy to spade up one shovelful of dirt and drop it onto the tarp. But by about the thirtieth shovelful, he was getting tired.

"This is insane. We need a backhoe," he said, wiping his forehead.

"You can rest if you want," James said coolly.

Phil understood. James was the backhoe. He was stronger than anyone Phil had ever seen. He pitched up shovelful after shovelful of dirt without even straining. He made it look like fun.

"*Why* don't we have you on any of the teams at school?" Phil said, leaning heavily on his shovel.

"I prefer individual sports. Like wrestling," James said and grinned, just for a moment, up at Phil. It was the kind of locker-room remark that couldn't be misunderstood from one guy to another. He meant wrestling with, for instance, Jacklyn and Michaela.

And, just at that particular moment, Phil couldn't help grinning back. He couldn't summon up any righteous disapproval.

Even with James, it took a long time to dig the hole. It was wider than Phil would have thought necessary. When his shovel finally *chunked* on something solid, he found out why.

"It's the vault," James said.

"*What* vault?"

"The burial vault. They put the coffin inside it so it doesn't get crushed if the ground collapses. Get out and hand me the crowbar."

Phil climbed out of the hole and gave him the crowbar. He could see the vault now. It was made of unfinished concrete and he guessed that it was just a rectangular box with a lid. James was prying the lid off with the crowbar.

"There," James said, with an explosive grunt as he lifted the lid and slid it, by degrees, behind the concrete box. That was why the hole was so wide, to accommodate the lid on one side and James on the other.

And now, looking straight down into the hole, Phil could see the casket. A huge spray of slightly crushed yellow roses was on top.

James was breathing hard, but Phil didn't think it was with exertion. His own lungs felt as if they were being squeezed flat, and his heart was thudding hard enough to shake his body.

"Oh, God," he said quietly and with no particular emphasis.

James looked up. "Yeah. This is it." He pushed the roses down toward the foot of the casket. Then, in what seemed like slow motion to Phillip, he began unfastening latches on the casket's side.

When they were unfastened, he paused for just an instant, both hands flat on the smooth surface of the casket. Then he lifted the upper panel, and Phillip could see what was inside.

CHAPTER 12

Poppy was lying there on the white velvet lining, eyes shut. She looked very pale and strangely beautiful— but was she dead?

"Wake up," James said. He put his hand on hers. Phillip had the feeling that he was calling with his mind as well as his voice.

There was an agonizingly long minute while nothing happened. James put his other hand under Poppy's neck, lifting her just slightly. "Poppy, it's time. Wake up. Wake up."

Poppy's eyelashes fluttered.

Something jarred violently in Phillip. He wanted to give a yell of victory and pound the grass. He also wanted to run away. Finally he just collapsed by the graveside, his knees giving out altogether.

"Come on, Poppy. Get up. We have to go." James was speaking in a gentle, insistent voice, as if he were talking to someone coming out of anesthesia.

Which was exactly how Poppy looked. As Phil watched with fascination and awe and dread, she blinked and rolled her head a little, then opened her eyes. She shut them again almost immediately, but James went on talking to her, and the next time she opened them they stayed open.

Then, with James urging her gently, she sat up.

"Poppy," Phil said. An involuntary outburst. His chest was swelling, burning.

Poppy looked up, then squinted and turned immediately from the beam of the flashlight. She looked annoyed.

"Come on," James said, helping her out of the open half of the casket. It wasn't hard; Poppy was small. With James holding her arm, she stood on the closed half of the casket, and Phil reached into the hole and pulled her up.

Then, with something like a convulsion, he hugged her.

When he pulled back, she blinked at him. A slight frown puckered her forehead. She licked her index finger and drew the wet finger across his cheek.

"You're filthy," she said.

She could talk. She didn't have red eyes and a chalky face. She was really alive.

Weak with relief, Phil hugged her again. "Oh, God, Poppy, you're okay. You're okay."

He barely noticed that she wasn't hugging him back.

James scrambled out of the hole. "How do you feel, Poppy?" he said. Not a politeness. A quiet, probing question.

Poppy looked at him, and then at Phillip. "I feel . . . fine."

"That's good," James said, still watching her as if she were a six-hundred-pound schizophrenic gorilla.

"I feel . . . hungry," Poppy said, in the same pleasant, musical voice she'd used before.

Phil blinked.

"Why don't you come over here, Phil?" James said, making a gesture behind him.

Phil was beginning to feel very uneasy. Poppy was . . . could she be *smelling* him? Not loud, wet sniffs, but the delicate little sniffs of a cat. She was nosing around his shoulder.

"Phil, I think you should come around over here," James said, with more emphasis. But what happened next happened too quickly for Phil even to start moving.

Delicate hands clenched like steel around his biceps. Poppy smiled at him with very sharp teeth, then darted like a striking cobra for his throat.

I'm going to die, Phil thought with a curious calm. He couldn't fight her. But her first strike missed. The sharp teeth grazed his throat like two burning pokers.

"No, you don't," James said. He looped an arm around Poppy's waist, lifting her off Phil.

Poppy gave a disappointed wail. As Phil struggled to his feet, she watched him the way a cat watches an interesting insect. Never taking her eyes off him, not even when James spoke to her.

"That's your brother, Phil. Your twin brother. Remember?"

Poppy just stared at Phil with hugely dilated pupils. Phil realized that she looked not only pale and beautiful but dazed and starving.

"My brother? One of our kind?" Poppy said, sounding puzzled. Her nostrils quivered and her lips parted. "He doesn't smell like it."

"No, he's not one of our kind, but he's not for biting, either. You're going to have to wait just a little while to feed." To Phillip, he said, "Let's get this hole filled in, fast."

Phillip couldn't move at first. Poppy was still watching him in that dreamy but intense way. She stood there in the darkness in her best white dress, supple as a lily, with her hair falling around her face. And she looked at him with the eyes of a jaguar.

She wasn't human anymore. She was something *other*. She'd said it herself, she and James were of one kind and Phil was something different. She belonged to the Night World now.

Oh, God, maybe we should just have let her die, Phil thought, and picked up a shovel with loose and trembling hands. James had already gotten the lid back on the vault. Phil shoveled dirt on it without looking at where it landed. His head wobbled as if his neck were a pipe cleaner.

"Don't be an *idiot*," a voice said, and hard fingers closed on Phil's wrist briefly. Through a blur, Phil saw James.

"She's not better off dead. She's just confused right now. This is *temporary*, all right?"

The words were brusque, but Phil felt a tiny surge of comfort. Maybe James was right. Life was good, in whatever form. And Poppy had chosen this.

Still, she'd changed, and only time would tell how much.

One thing—Phil had made the mistake of thinking that vampires were like humans. He'd gotten so comfortable with James that he'd almost forgotten their differences.

He wouldn't make that mistake again.

Poppy felt wonderful—in almost every way.

She felt secret and strong. She felt poetic and full of possibility. She felt as if she'd sloughed off her old body like a snake shedding its skin, to reveal a fresh new body underneath.

And she knew, without being quite sure how she knew, that she didn't have cancer.

It was gone, the terrible thing that had been running wild inside her. Her new body had killed it and absorbed it somehow. Or maybe it was just that every cell that made up Poppy North, every molecule, had changed.

However it was, she felt vibrant and healthy. Not just better than she had before she'd gotten the cancer, but better than she could remember feeling in her life. She was strangely aware of her own body, and her muscles and joints all seemed to be working in a way that was sweet and almost magical.

The only problem was that she was hungry. It was taking all her willpower not to pounce on the blond guy in the hole. Phillip. Her brother.

She *knew* he was her brother, but he was also human and she could sense the rich stuff, lush with life, that was coursing through his veins. The electrifying fluid she needed to survive.

So jump him, part of her mind whispered. Poppy frowned and tried to wiggle away from the thought. She felt something in her mouth nudging her lower lip, and she poked her thumb at it instinctively.

It was a tooth. A delicate curving tooth. Both her canine teeth were long and pointed and very sensitive.

How weird. She rubbed at the new teeth gently, then cautiously explored them with her tongue. She pressed them against her lip.

After a moment they shrank to normal size. If she thought about humans full of blood like berries, they grew again.

Hey, look what I can do!

But she didn't bother the two grimy boys who were filling in the hole. She glanced around and tried to distract herself instead.

Strange—it didn't really seem to be either day or night. Maybe there was an eclipse. It was too dim to be daytime, but far too bright for nighttime. She could see the leaves on the maple trees and the gray Spanish moss hanging from the oak trees. Tiny moths were fluttering around the moss, and she could see their pale wings.

When she looked at the sky, she got a shock. There was something floating there, a giant round thing that blazed with silvery light. Poppy thought of spaceships, of alien worlds, before she realized the truth.

It was the *moon*. Just an ordinary full moon. And the reason it looked so big and throbbing with light was that she had night vision. That was why she could see the moths, too.

All her senses were keen. Delicious smells wafted by her, the smells of small burrowing animals and fluttering dainty birds. On the wind came a tantalizing hint of rabbit.

And she could *hear* things. Once she whipped her head around as a dog barked right beside her. Then she realized that it was far away, outside the cemetery. It only sounded close.

I'll bet I can run fast, too, she thought. Her legs felt tingly. She wanted to go running out into the lovely, gloriously-scented night, to be one with it. She was *part* of it now.

James, she said. And the strange thing was that she said it without saying it out loud. It was something she knew how to do without thinking.

James looked up from his shoveling. *Hang on,* he said the same way. *We're almost done, kiddo.*

Then you'll teach me to hunt?

He nodded, just slightly. His hair was falling over his forehead and he looked adorably grubby. Poppy felt as if she'd never really seen him before—because now she was seeing him with new senses. James wasn't just silky brown hair and enigmatic gray eyes and a lithe-muscled body. He was the smell of winter rain and the sound of his predator's heartbeat and the silvery aura of power she could feel around him. She could sense his mind, lean and tiger-tough but somehow gentle and almost wistful at the same time.

We're hunting partners now, she told him eagerly, and he smiled an acknowledgment. But underneath she felt that he was worried. He was either sad or anxious about something, something he was keeping from her.

She couldn't think about it. She didn't feel hungry anymore . . . she felt strange. As if she was having trouble getting enough air.

James and Phillip were shaking out the tarps, unrolling strips of fresh sod to cover the grave. Her grave. Funny she hadn't really thought about that before. She'd been lying in a grave—she ought to feel repulsed or scared.

She didn't. She didn't remember being in there at all—didn't remember anything from the time she'd fallen asleep in her bedroom until she'd woken up with James calling her.

Except a dream . . .

"Okay," James said. He was folding up a tarp. "We can go. How're you feeling?"

"Ummm . . . a little weird. I can't get a deep breath."

"Neither can I," Phil said. He was breathing hard and

wiping his forehead. "I didn't know grave digging was such hard work."

James gave Poppy a searching look. "Do you think you can make it back to my apartment?"

"Hmm? I guess." Poppy didn't actually know what he was talking about. Make it how? And why should going to his apartment help her to breathe?

"I've got a couple of safe donors there in the building," James said. "I don't really want you out on the streets, and I think you'll make it there okay."

Poppy didn't ask what he meant. She was having trouble thinking clearly.

James wanted her to hide in the backseat of his car. Poppy refused. She needed to sit up front and to feel the night air on her face.

"Okay," James said at last. "But at least sort of cover your face with your arm. I'll drive on back roads. You *can't* be seen, Poppy."

There didn't seem to be anyone on the streets to see her. The air whipping her cheeks was cool and good, but it didn't help her breathing. No matter how she tried, she couldn't seem to get a proper breath.

I'm hyperventilating, she thought. Her heart was racing, her lips and tongue felt parchment-dry. And still she had the feeling of being air-starved.

What's *happening* to me?

Then the pain started.

Agonizing seizures in her muscles—like the cramps she used to get when she went out for track in junior high. Vaguely, through the pain, she remembered something the P.E. teacher had said. *"The cramps come when your muscles don't get enough blood. A charley horse is a clump of muscles starving to death."*

Oh, it *hurt.* It *hurt.* She couldn't even call to James for help, now; all she could do was hang on to the car door and try to breathe. She was whooping and wheezing, but it wasn't any good.

Cramps everywhere—and now she was so dizzy that she saw the world through sparkling lights.

She was dying. Something had gone terribly wrong. She felt as if she were underwater, trying desperately to claw her way to oxygen—only there *was* no oxygen.

And then she saw the way.

Or smelled it, actually. The car was stopped at a red light. Poppy's head and shoulders were out the window by now— and suddenly she caught a whiff of life.

Life. What she needed. She didn't think, she simply acted. With one motion she threw the car door open and plunged out.

She heard Phil's shout behind her and James's shout in her head. She ignored both of them. Nothing mattered except stopping the pain.

She grabbed for the man on the sidewalk the way a drowning swimmer grabs at a rescuer. Instinctively. He was tall and strong for a human. He was wearing a dark sweatsuit and a bomber jacket. His face was stubbly and his skin wasn't exactly clean, but that wasn't important. She wasn't interested in the container, only in the lovely sticky red stuff inside.

This time her strike was perfectly accurate. Her wonderful teeth extended like claws and stabbed into the man's throat. Puncturing him like one of those old-fashioned bottle openers. He struggled a little and then went limp.

And then she was drinking, her throat drenched in copper-sweetness. Sheer animal hunger took over as she tapped his veins. The liquid filling her mouth was wild and raw and primal and every swallow gave her new life.

She drank and drank, and felt the pain disappear. In its place was a euphoric lightness. When she paused to breathe, she could feel her lungs swell with cool, blessed air.

She bent to drink again, to suck, lap, tipple. The man had a clear bubbling stream inside him, and she wanted it all.

That was when James pulled her head back.

He spoke both aloud and in her mind and his voice was collected but intense. "Poppy, I'm sorry. I'm sorry. It was my fault. I shouldn't have made you wait so long. But you've had enough now. You can stop."

Oh . . . confusion. Poppy was peripherally aware of Phillip, her brother Phillip, looking on in horror. James said she *could* stop, but that didn't mean she had to. She didn't *want* to. The man wasn't fighting at all now. He seemed to be unconscious.

She bent down again. James pulled her back up almost roughly.

"Listen," he said. His eyes were level, but his voice was hard. "This is the time you can choose, Poppy. Do you *really* want to kill?"

The words shocked her back to awareness. To kill . . . that was the way to get power, she knew. Blood was power and life and energy and food and drink. If she drained this man like squeezing an orange, she would have the power of his very essence. Who knew what she might be able to do then?

But . . . he was a man, not an orange. A human being. She'd been one of those once.

Slowly, reluctantly, she lifted herself off the man, and James let out a long breath. He patted her shoulder and sat down on the sidewalk as if too tired to stand up right then.

Phil was slumped against the wall of the nearest building.

He was appalled, and Poppy could feel it. She could even pick up words he was thinking—words like *ghastly* and *amoral.* A whole sentence that went something like "Is it worth it to save her life if she's lost her soul?"

James jerked around to look at him, and Poppy could feel the silver flare of his anger. "You just don't get it, do you?" he said savagely. "She could have attacked *you* anytime, but she didn't, even though she was dying. You don't know what the bloodlust feels like. It's not like being thirsty—it's like suffocating. Your cells start to die from oxygen starvation, because your own blood can't carry oxygen to them. It's the worst pain there is, but she didn't go after you to make it stop."

Phillip looked staggered. He stared at Poppy, then held out a hand uncertainly.

"I'm sorry. . . ."

"Forget it," James said shortly. He turned his back on Phil and examined the man. Poppy could feel him extend his mind. "I'm telling him to forget this," he said to Poppy. "All he needs is some rest, and he might as well do that right here. See, the wounds are already healing."

Poppy saw, but she couldn't feel happy. She knew Phil still disapproved of her. Not just for something she'd done, but for what she *was*.

What's happened to me? she asked James, throwing herself into his arms. *Have I turned into something awful?*

He held her fiercely. *You're just different. Not awful. Phil's a jerk.*

She wanted to laugh at that. But she could feel a tremor of sadness behind his protective love. It was the same anxious sadness she'd sensed in him earlier. James didn't like being a predator, and now he'd made Poppy one, too. Their plan had succeeded brilliantly—and Poppy would never be the old Poppy North again.

And although she could hear his thoughts, it wasn't exactly like the total immersion when they'd exchanged blood. They might not ever have that togetherness again.

"There wasn't any other choice," Poppy said stoutly, and she said it aloud. "We did what we had to do. Now we have to make the best of it."

You're a brave girl. Did I ever tell you that?

No. And if you did, I don't mind hearing it again.

But they drove to James's apartment building in silence, with Phil's depression weighing heavily in the backseat.

"Look, you can take the car back to your house," James said as he unloaded the equipment and Poppy's clothes into his carport. "I don't want to bring Poppy anywhere near there, and I don't want to leave her alone."

Phil glanced up at the dark two-story building as if something had just struck him. Then he cleared his throat. Poppy knew why—James's apartment was a notorious place, and she'd never been allowed to visit it at night. Apparently Phil still had some brotherly concern for his vampire sister. "You, uh, can't just take her to your parents' house?"

"How many times do I have to explain? No, I can't take her to my parents, because my parents don't know she's a vampire. Right at the moment she's an illegal vampire, a renegade, which means she's got to be kept a secret until I can straighten things out—somehow."

"How—" Phil stopped and shook his head. "Okay. Not tonight. We'll talk about it later."

"No, 'we' won't," James said harshly. "You're not a part of this anymore. It's up to Poppy and me. All you need to do is go back and live your normal life and keep your mouth shut."

Phil started to say something else, then caught himself. He took the keys from James. Then he looked at Poppy.

"I'm glad you're alive. I love you," he said.

Poppy knew that he wanted to hug her, but something kept both of them back. There was an emptiness in Poppy's chest.

"Bye, Phil," she said, and he got in the car and left.

CHAPTER 13

H e doesn't understand," Poppy said softly as James unlocked the door to his apartment. "He just hasn't grasped that you're risking your life, too."

The apartment was very bare and utilitarian. High ceilings and spacious rooms announced that it was expensive, but there wasn't much furniture. In the living room there was a low, square couch, a desk with a computer, and a couple of Oriental-looking pictures on the wall. And books. Cardboard boxes of books stacked in the corners.

Poppy turned to face James directly. "Jamie . . . *I* understand."

James smiled at her. He was sweaty and dirty and tired-looking. But his expression said Poppy made it all worthwhile.

"Don't blame Phil," he said, with a gesture of dismissal. "He's actually handling things pretty well. I've never broken cover to a human before, but I think most of them would run screaming and never come back. He's *trying* to cope, at least."

Poppy nodded and dropped the subject. James was tired, which meant they should go to sleep. She picked up the duffel bag that Phil had packed with her clothes and headed for the bathroom.

She didn't change right away, though. She was too fascinated by her own reflection in the mirror. So this was what a vampire Poppy looked like.

She was prettier, she noted with absent satisfaction. The four freckles on her nose were gone. Her skin was creamy-pale, like an advertisement for face cream. Her eyes were green as jewels. Her hair was wind-blown into riotous curls, metallic-copper.

I don't look like something that sits on a buttercup anymore, she thought. I look wild and dangerous and exotic. Like a model. Like a rock star. Like James.

She leaned forward to examine her teeth, poking at the canines to make them grow. Then she jerked back, gasping.

Her eyes. She hadn't realized. Oh, God, no wonder Phil had been scared. When she did that, when her teeth extended, her eyes went silvery-green, uncanny. Like the eyes of a hunting cat.

All at once she was overcome by terror. She had to cling to the sink to stay on her feet.

I don't want it, I don't want it. . . .

Oh, *deal* with it, girl. Stop whining. So what did you expect to look like, Shirley Temple? You're a hunter now. And your eyes go silver and blood tastes like cherry preserves. And that's all there is to it, and the other choice was resting in peace. So *deal.*

Gradually her breathing slowed. In the next few minutes something happened inside her; she *did* deal. She found . . . acceptance. It felt like something giving way in her throat and her stomach. She wasn't weird and dreamy now, as she'd been when she had first awakened in the cemetery; she could think clearly about her situation. And she could accept it.

And I did it without running to James, she thought suddenly, startled. I don't need him to comfort me or tell me it's okay. I can *make* it okay, myself.

Maybe that was what happened when you faced the very worst thing in the world. She'd lost her family and her old life and maybe even her childhood, but she'd found herself. And that would have to do.

She pulled the white dress over her head and changed into a T-shirt and sweatpants. Then she walked out to James, head high.

He was in the bedroom, lying on a full-sized bed made up with light brown sheets. He was still wearing his dirty clothes, and he had one arm crooked over his eyes. When Poppy came in, he stirred.

"I'll go sleep on the couch," he said.

"No, you won't," Poppy said firmly. She flopped on the bed beside him. "You're dead tired. And I know I'm safe with you."

James grinned without moving his arm. "Because I'm dead tired?"

"Because I've always been safe with you." She knew that. Even when she'd been a human and her blood must have tempted him, she'd been safe.

She looked at him as he lay there, brown hair ruffled, body lax, Adidas unlaced and caked with soil. She found his elbows endearing.

"I forgot to mention something before," she said. "I only realized I forgot when I was . . . going to sleep. I forgot to mention that I love you."

James sat up. "You only forgot to say it with words."

Poppy felt a smile tugging at her lips. That was the amazing thing, the only purely good thing about what had happened to her. She and James had come together. Their relationship had changed—but it still had everything she'd valued in their old relationship. The understanding, the camaraderie. Now on top of that was the new excitement of discovering each other as more than best friends.

And she'd found the part of him that she had never been able to reach before. She knew his secrets, knew him inside out. Humans could never know each other that way. They could never really get into another person's head. All the talking in the world couldn't even prove that you and the other person both saw the same color red.

And if she and James never merged like two drops of water again, she would always be able to touch his mind.

A little shy, she leaned against him, resting on his shoulder. In all the times they'd been close, they'd never kissed or been romantic. For now, just sitting here like this was enough, just feeling James breathe and hearing his heart and absorbing his warmth. And his arm around her shoulders was almost *too* much, almost too intense to bear, but at the same time it was safe and peaceful.

It was like a song, one of those sweet, wrenching songs that makes the hair on your arms stand up. That makes you want to throw yourself on the floor and just bawl. Or fall backward and surrender to the music utterly. One of *those* songs.

James cupped her hand, brought it to his lips, and kissed the palm.

I told you. You don't love somebody because of their looks or their clothes or their car. You love them because they sing a song that nobody but you can understand.

Poppy's heart swelled until it hurt.

Aloud she said, "We always understood the same song, even when we were little."

"In the Night World there's this idea called the soulmate principle. It says that every person has one soulmate out there, just one. And that person is perfect for you and is your destiny.

The problem being that almost nobody ever *finds* their soul-mate, just because of distance. So most people go through their whole lives feeling not complete."

"I think it's the truth. I *always* knew you were perfect for me."

"Not *always*."

"Oh, yes. Since I was five. I knew."

"I'd have known you were perfect for me—except that everything I'd been taught said it was hopeless." He cleared his throat and added, "That *is* why I went out with Michaela and those other girls, you know. I didn't care about them. I could get close to them without breaking the law."

"I know," Poppy said. "I mean—I think I always knew it was something like that, underneath." She added, "James? What am I now?" Some things she could tell instinctively; she could feel them in her blood. But she wanted to know more, and she knew James understood why. This was her life now. She had to learn the rules.

"Well." He settled against the headboard, head tilted back as she rested under his chin. "You're pretty much like me. Except for not being able to age or have families, made vampires are basically like the lamia." He shifted. "Let's see. You already know about being able to see and hear better than humans. And you're a whiz at reading minds."

"Not everybody's mind."

"No vampire can read everybody's mind. Lots of times all I

get is a sort of general feeling for what people are thinking. The only certain way to make a connection is to—" James opened his mouth and clicked his teeth. Poppy giggled as the sound traveled through her skull.

"And how often do I have to—?" She clicked her own teeth.

"Feed." She felt James getting serious. "About once a day on average. Otherwise you'll go into the bloodlust. You can eat human food if you want, but there's no nutrition in it. Blood is everything for us."

"And the more blood, the more power."

"Basically, yes."

"Tell me about power. Can we—well, what can we do?"

"We have more control over our bodies than humans. We can heal from almost any kind of injury—except from wood. Wood can hurt us, even kill us." He snorted. "So there's one thing the movies have right—a wooden stake through the heart will, in fact, kill a vampire. So will burning."

"Can we change into animals?"

"I've never met any vampire that powerful. But theoretically it's possible for us, and shapeshifters and werewolves do it all the time."

"Change into mist?"

"I've never even met a shapeshifter who could do that."

Poppy thumped the bed with her heel. "And obviously we don't have to sleep in coffins."

"No, and we don't need native earth, either. Myself, I prefer a Sealy Posturepedic, but if you'd like some dirt . . ."

Poppy elbowed him. "Um, can we cross running water?"

"Sure. And we can walk into people's homes without being invited, and roll in garlic if we don't mind losing friends. Anything else?"

"Yes. Tell me about the Night World." It was her home now.

"Did I tell you about the clubs? We have clubs in every big city. In a lot of small ones, too."

"What kind of clubs?"

"Well, some are just dives, and some are like cafés, and some are like nightclubs, and some are like lodges—those are mostly for adults. I know one for kids that's just a big old warehouse with skate ramps built in. You can hang out and skateboard. And there are poetry slams every week at the Black Iris."

Black iris, Poppy thought. That reminded her of something. Something unpleasant . . .

What she said was, "That's a funny name."

"All the clubs are named for flowers. Black flowers are the symbols of the Night People." He rotated his wrist to show her his watch. An analog watch, with a black iris in the center of the face. "See?"

"Yeah. You know, I noticed that black thing, but I never really looked at it before. I think I assumed it was Mickey Mouse."

He rapped her lightly on the nose in reproof. "This is serious business, kid. One of these will identify you to other Night People—even if they're as stupid as a werewolf."

"You don't like werewolves?"

"They're great if you like double-digit IQs."

"But you let them in the clubs."

"Some clubs. Night People may not marry out of their own kind, but they all mix: lamia, made vampires, werewolves, both kinds of witches . . ."

Poppy, who had been playing at intertwining their fingers in different ways, shifted curiously. "What's both kinds of witches?"

"Oh . . . there's the kind that know about their heritage and have been trained, and the kind that don't. That second kind are what humans call psychics. Sometimes they just have latent powers, and some of them aren't even psychic enough to *find* the Night World, so they don't get in."

Poppy nodded. "Okay. Got it. But what if a human walks into one of those clubs?"

"Nobody would let them. The clubs aren't what you'd call conspicuous, and they're always guarded."

"But if they *did* . . ."

James shrugged. His voice was suddenly bleak. "They'd be killed. Unless somebody wanted to pick them up as a toy or pawn. That means a human who's basically brainwashed—who lives with vampires but doesn't know it because of the mind control. Sort of like a sleepwalker. I had a nanny once . . ." His voice trailed off, and Poppy could feel his distress.

"You can tell me about it later." She didn't want him ever to be hurt again.

"M'm." He sounded sleepy. Poppy settled herself more comfortably against him.

It was amazing, considering her last experience going to sleep, that she could even shut her eyes. But she could. She was with her soulmate, so what could go wrong? Nothing could hurt her here.

Phil was having trouble shutting his eyes.

Every time he did, he saw Poppy. Poppy asleep in the casket. Poppy watching him with a hungry cat's gaze. Poppy lifting her head from that guy's throat to show a mouth stained as if she'd been eating berries.

She wasn't human anymore.

And just because he'd known all along that she wouldn't be didn't make it any easier to accept.

He couldn't—he *couldn't*—condone jumping on people and tearing up their throats for dinner. And he wasn't sure that it was any better to charm people and bite them and then hypnotize them to forget it. The whole system was scary on some deep level.

Maybe James had been right—humans just couldn't deal with the idea that there was somebody higher on the food chain. They'd lost touch with their caveman ancestors, who knew what it was like to be hunted. They thought all that primal stuff was behind them.

Could Phillip tell them a thing or two.

The bottom line was that he couldn't accept, and Poppy couldn't change. And the only thing that made it bearable was that somehow he loved her anyway.

Poppy woke in the dim, curtained bedroom the next day to find the other half of the bed empty. She wasn't alarmed, though. Instinctively she reached out with her mind, and . . . there. James was in the kitchenette.

She felt . . . energetic. Like a puppy straining to be let loose in a field. But as soon as she walked into the living room, she felt that her powers were weaker. And her eyes hurt. She squinted toward the painful brightness of a window.

"It's the sun," James said. "Inhibits all vampire powers, remember?" He went over to the window and closed the curtains—they were the blackout type, like the ones in the bedroom. The midafternoon sunshine was cut off. "That should help a little—but you'd better stay inside today until it gets dark. New vampires are more sensitive."

Poppy caught something behind his words. "You're going out?"

"I have to." He grimaced. "There's something I forgot— my cousin Ash is supposed to show up this week. I've got to get my parents to head him off."

"I didn't know you had a cousin."

He winced again. "I've got lots, actually. They're back East in a safe town—a whole town that's controlled by the Night World. Most of them are okay, but not Ash."

"What's wrong with him?"

"He's crazy. Also cold-blooded, ruthless—"

"You sound like Phil describing you."

"No, Ash is the real thing. The ultimate vampire. He doesn't care about anybody but himself, and he loves to make trouble."

Poppy was prepared to love all James's cousins for his sake, but she had to agree that Ash sounded dangerous.

"I wouldn't trust anyone to know about you just now," James said, "and Ash is out of the question. I'm going to tell my parents he can't come here, that's all."

And then what do we do? Poppy thought. She couldn't stay hidden forever. She belonged to the Night World—but the Night World wouldn't accept her.

There had to be some solution—and she could only hope that she and James would find it.

"Don't be gone too long," she said, and he kissed her on the forehead, which was nice. As if it was getting to be a habit.

When he was gone, she took a shower and put on clean clothes. Good old Phil—he'd slipped in her favorite jeans. Then she made herself putter around the apartment, because she didn't want to sit and *think*. Nobody should have to think on the day after their own funeral.

The phone sat beside the square couch and mocked her. She found herself resisting the impulse to pick it up so often that her arm ached.

But who could she call? Nobody. Not even Phil, because what if somebody overheard him? What if her mother answered?

No, no, don't think about Mom, you idiot.

But it was too late. She was overwhelmed, suddenly, by a desperate *need* to hear her mother's voice. Just to hear a "hello." She knew she couldn't say anything herself. She just needed to establish that her mom still existed.

She punched the phone number in without giving herself time to think. She counted rings. One, two, three . . .

"Hello?"

It was her mother's voice. And it was already over, and it wasn't enough. Poppy sat trying to breathe, with tears running down her face. She hung there, wringing the phone cord, listening to the faint buzz on the other end. Like a prisoner in court waiting to hear her sentence.

"Hello? Hello." Her mother's voice was flat and tired. Not acerbic. Prank phone calls were no big deal when you'd just lost your daughter.

Then a click signaled disconnection.

Poppy clutched the earpiece to her chest and cried,

rocking slightly. At last she put it back on the cradle.

Well, she wouldn't do *that* again. It was worse than not being able to hear her mother at all. And it didn't help her with reality, either. It gave her a dizzy Twilight Zone feeling to think that her mom was at home, and everybody was at home, and *Poppy wasn't there.* Life was going on in that house, but she wasn't part of it anymore. She couldn't just walk in, any more than she could walk into some strange family's house.

You're really a glutton for punishment, aren't you? Why don't you stop thinking about this and *do* something distracting?

She was snooping through James's file cabinet when the apartment door opened.

Because she heard the metallic jingle of a key, she assumed it was James. But then, even before she turned, she knew it *wasn't* James. It wasn't James's mind.

She turned and saw a boy with ash blond hair.

He was very good looking, built about like James, but a little taller, and maybe a year older. His hair was longish. His face had a nice shape, clean-cut features, and wicked slightly tilted eyes.

But that wasn't why she was staring at him.

He gave her a flashing smile.

"I'm Ash," he said. "Hi."

Poppy was still staring. "You were in my dream," she said. "You said, 'Bad magic happens.'"

"So you're a psychic?"

"What?"

"Your dreams come true?"

"Not usually." Poppy suddenly got hold of herself. "Listen, um, I don't know how you got in—"

He jingled a key ring at her. "Aunt Maddy gave me these. James told you to keep me out, I bet."

Poppy decided that the best defense was a good offense. "Now, why would he tell me that?" she said, and folded her arms over her chest.

He gave her a wicked, laughing glance. His eyes looked hazel in this light, almost golden. "I'm bad," he said simply.

Poppy tried to plaster a look of righteous disapproval— like Phil's—on her face. It didn't work very well. "Does James know you're here? Where *is* he?"

"I have no idea. Aunt Maddy gave me the keys at lunch, and then she went out on some interior decorating job. What did you dream about?"

Poppy just shook her head. She was trying to think. Presumably, James was wandering around in search of his mother right now. Once he found her he'd find out that Ash was over here, and then he'd come back fast. Which meant . . . well, Poppy supposed it meant she should keep Ash occupied until James arrived.

But how? She'd never really practiced being winsome and adorable with guys. And she was worried about talking too much. She might give herself away as a new vampire.

Oh, well. When in doubt, shut your eyes and jump right in.

"Know any good werewolf jokes?" she said.

He laughed. He had a nice laugh, and his eyes weren't hazel after all. They were gray, like James's.

"You haven't told me your name yet, little dreamer," he said.

"Poppy," Poppy said and immediately wished she hadn't. What if Mrs. Rasmussen had mentioned that one of James's little friends called Poppy had just died? To conceal her nervousness, she got up to close the door.

"Good lamia name," he said. "I don't like this yuppy thing of taking on human names, do you? I've got three sisters, and they all have regular old-fashioned names. Rowan, Kestrel, Jade. My dad would burst a blood vessel if one of them suddenly wanted to call herself 'Susan.'"

"Or 'Maddy'?" Poppy asked, intrigued despite herself.

"Huh? It's short for Madder."

Poppy wasn't sure what madder was. A plant, she thought.

"Of course I'm not saying anything against James," Ash said, and it was perfectly clear from his voice that he *was* saying something against James. "Things are different for you guys in California. You have to mix more with humans; you have to be more careful. So if naming yourself after vermin makes it easier . . ." He shrugged.

"Oh, yeah, they're vermin all right," Poppy said at random. She was thinking, He's playing with me. Isn't he playing with me?

She had the sinking feeling that he knew everything. Agitation made her need to move. She headed for James's stereo center.

"So you like any vermin music?" she said. "Techno? Acid jazz? Trip-hop? Jungle?" She waved a vinyl record at him. "This is some serious jump-up jungle." He blinked. "Oh, and this is great industrial noise. And this is a real good acid house stomper with a sort of madcore edge to it. . . ."

She had him on the defensive now. Nobody could stop Poppy when she got going like this. She widened her eyes at him and blathered on, looking as fey as she knew how.

"And I say freestyle's coming *back*. Completely underground, so far, but on the *rise*. Now, Euro-dance, on the other hand . . ."

Ash was sitting on the square couch, long legs stretched out in front of him. His eyes were deep blue and slightly glazed.

"Sweetheart," he said finally, "I hate to interrupt. But you and I need to talk."

Poppy was too clever to ask him what about. ". . . these sort of eternal void keys and troll groaning sounds that make you want to ask, 'Is anybody out there?'" she finished, and then she had to breathe. Ash jumped in.

"We *really* have to talk," he said. "Before James gets back."

There was no way to evade him now. Poppy's mouth was dry. He leaned forward, his eyes a clear blue-green like tropical waters. And, yes, they really *do* change color, Poppy thought.

"It's not your fault," he said.

"What?"

It's not your fault. That you can't shield your mind. You'll learn how to do it, he said, and Poppy only realized halfway through that he wasn't saying it out loud.

Oh . . . *spit.* She should have thought of that. Should have been concentrating on veiling her thoughts. She tried to do it now.

"Listen, don't bother. I know that you're not lamia. You're made, and you're illegal. James has been a bad boy."

Since there was no point in denying it, Poppy lifted her chin and narrowed her eyes at him. "So you know. So what are you going to do about it?"

"That depends."

"On what?"

He smiled. "On you."

CHAPTER 14

Y ou see, I like James," Ash said. "I think he's a little soft on vermin, but I don't want to see him in trouble. I certainly don't want to see him *dead*."

Poppy felt the way she had last night when her body was starving for air. She was frozen, too still to breathe.

"I mean, do *you* want him dead?" Ash asked, as if it were the most reasonable question in the world.

Poppy shook her head.

"Well, then," Ash said.

Poppy got a breath at last. "What are you *saying*?" Then, without waiting for him to answer, she said, "You're saying that they're going to kill him if they find out about me. But they don't *have* to find out about me. Unless you tell them."

Ash glanced at his fingernails thoughtfully. He made a face to show that this was as painful for him as it was for her.

"Let's go over the facts," he said. "You are, in fact, a former human."

"Oh, yeah, I was a vermin, all right."

He gave her a droll look. "Don't take that so seriously. It's what you are now that counts. But James did, in fact, change you without clearing it with *anybody*. Right? And he did, in fact, break cover and tell you about the Night World before you were changed. Right?"

"How do you know? Maybe he just changed me without telling me a thing."

He shook a finger. "Ah, but James wouldn't do that. He's got these radical permissive ideas about humans having free will."

"If you know all about it, why ask me?" Poppy said tensely. "And if you've got a point—"

"The point is that he's committed at least two capital offenses. Three, I bet." He flashed the wild, handsome smile again. "He must have been in love with you to have done the rest."

Something swelled in Poppy like a bird trapped in her rib cage and trying to get out. She blurted, "I don't see how you people can make laws about not falling in love! It's insane."

"But don't you see *why*? You're the perfect example. Because of love, James told you and then he changed you. If he'd had the sense to squash his feelings for you in the beginning, the whole thing would have been nipped in the bud."

L. J. SMITH

"But what if you *can't* squash it? You can't *force* people to stop feeling."

"Of course not," Ash said, and Poppy stopped dead. She stared at him.

His lips curved and he beckoned to her. "I'll tell you a secret. The Elders know they can't really legislate how you *feel*. What they can do is terrorize you so that you don't dare show your feelings—ideally, so you can't even admit them to yourself."

Poppy settled back. She'd seldom felt so at a loss. Talking to Ash made her head whirl, made her feel as if she were too young and stupid to be sure of *anything*.

She made a forlorn and helpless gesture. "But what do I do now? I can't change the past. . . ."

"No, but you can act in the present." He jumped to his feet in a lovely, graceful motion and began pacing. "Now. We have to think fast. Presumably everyone here thinks you're dead."

"Yes, but—"

"So the answer is simple. You have to get out of the area and stay out. Go someplace where you won't be recognized, where nobody will care if you're new or illegal. Witches. That's it! I've got some cross-cousins in Las Vegas that will put you up. The main thing is to leave *now*."

Poppy's head wasn't just whirling, it was *reeling*. She felt dizzy and physically sick, as if she'd just stepped off Space Mountain at Disneyland. "What? I don't even understand what you're talking about," she said feebly.

"I'll explain on the way. Come on, hurry! Do you have some clothes you want to take?"

Poppy planted her feet solidly on the floor. She shook her head to try and clear it. "Look, I don't know what you're saying, but I can't go *anywhere* right now. I have to wait for James."

"But don't you see?" Ash stopped his whirlwind pacing and rounded on her. His eyes were green and hypnotically brilliant. "That's just what you *can't* do. James can't even know where you're going."

"*What?*"

"Don't you *see?*" Ash said again. He spread his hands and spoke almost pityingly. "*You're* the only thing putting James in danger. As long as you're here, anybody can look at you and put the pieces together. You're circumstantial evidence that he's committed a crime."

Poppy understood that. "But I can just wait and James can go away with me. He would *want* that."

"But it wouldn't work," Ash said softly. "It doesn't matter where you go; whenever you're together, you're a danger to him. One look at you and any decent vampire can sense the truth."

Poppy's knees felt weak.

Ash spoke soberly. "I'm not saying that you'll be much safer yourself if you leave. You bring your own danger with you, because of what you are. But as long as you're away from

James, nobody can connect you with *him*. It's the only way to keep him safe. Do you see?"

"Yes. Yes, I see that now." The ground seemed to have disappeared beneath Poppy. She was falling, not into music, but into an icy dark void. There was nothing to hold on to.

"But, of course, it's a lot to expect, to ask you to give him up. You may not want to make that kind of sacrifice—"

Poppy's chin came up. She was blind and empty and giddy, but she spoke to Ash with utter contempt, spitting out the words. "After everything he sacrificed for me? What do you think I am?"

Ash bowed his head. "You're a brave one, little dreamer. I can't believe you were ever human." Then he looked up and spoke briskly. "So do you want to pack?"

"I don't have much," Poppy said, slowly, because moving and speaking hurt her. She walked toward the bedroom as if the floor was covered with broken glass. "Hardly anything. But I have to write a note for James."

"No, no," Ash said. "That's the last thing you want to do. Well, after all," he added as she swiveled slowly to look at him, "James being so noble and lovestruck and everything—if you let him know where you're going, he'll come right after you. And then where will you be?"

Poppy shook her head. "I . . . okay." Still shaking her head, she stumbled into the bedroom.

She wasn't going to argue with him anymore, but she wasn't going to take his advice, either. She shut the bedroom door and tried as hard as she could to shield her mind. She visualized a stone wall around her thoughts.

Stuffing her sweat pants and T-shirt and white dress into the duffel bag took thirty seconds. Then she found a book under the nightstand and a felt-tip pen in the drawer. She tore the flyleaf out of the book and scribbled rapidly.

Dear James,

I'm so sorry, but if I stay to explain this to you, I know you'll try to stop me. Ash has made me understand the truth—that as long as I stick around I'm putting your life in danger. And I just can't do that. If something happened to you because of me, I would die. I really would.

I'm going away now. Ash is taking me somewhere far away where you won't find me. Where they won't care what I am. I'll be safe there. You'll be safe here. And even if we're not together, we'll never really be apart.

I love you. I'll love you forever. But I have to do this.

Please tell Phil goodbye.

Your soulmate, Poppy

She was dripping tears onto the paper as she signed it.

She put the flyleaf on the pillow and went out to Ash.

"Oh, there, there," he said. "Don't cry. You're doing the right thing." He put an arm around her shoulders. Poppy was too miserable to shrug it off.

She looked at him. "One thing. Won't I be putting *you* in danger if I go with you? I mean, somebody might think *you* were the one who made me an illegal vampire."

He looked at her with wide, earnest eyes. They happened to be blue-violet at the moment.

"I'm willing to take that risk," he said. "I have a lot of respect for you."

James took the stairs two at a time, sending probing thoughts ahead of him and then refusing to believe what his own senses told him.

She had to be there. She *had* to be. . . .

He pounded on the door at the same time as he was thrusting the key into the lock. At the same time as he was shouting mentally.

Poppy! Poppy, answer me! Poppy!

And then, even with the door flung open and his own thoughts ricocheting off the emptiness in the apartment, he *still* didn't want to believe. He ran around, looking in every room, his heart thudding louder and louder in his chest. Her duffel bag was gone. Her clothes were gone. She was gone.

He ended up leaning against the glass of the living room window. He could see the street below, and there was no sign of Poppy.

No sign of Ash, either.

It was James's fault. He'd been following his mother's trail all afternoon, from decorating job to decorating job, trying to catch up with her. Only to find, once he did catch up, that Ash was already in El Camino, and had, in fact, been sent over to James's apartment hours ago. With a key.

Putting him alone with Poppy.

James had called the apartment immediately. No answer. He'd broken all speed limits getting back here. But he was too late.

Ash, you snake, he thought. If you hurt her, if you put one finger on her . . .

He found himself roving over the apartment again, looking for clues as to what had happened. Then, in the bedroom, he noticed something pale against the light brown of the pillowcase.

A note. He snatched it up and read it. And got colder and colder with every line. By the time he reached the end, he was made of ice and ready to kill.

There were little round splashes where the felt-tip pen had run. Tears. He was going to break one of Ash's bones for each one.

He folded the note carefully and put it in his pocket. Then

he took a few things from his closet and made a call on his cellular phone as he was walking down the stairs of the apartment building.

"Mom, it's me," he said at the beep of an answering machine. "I'm going to be gone for a few days. Something's come up. If you see Ash, leave me a message. I want to talk with him."

He didn't say please. He knew his voice was clipped and sharp. And he didn't care. He hoped his tone would scare her.

Just at the moment he felt ready to take on his mother and father and all the vampire Elders in the Night World. One stake for all of them.

He wasn't a child anymore. In the last week he'd been through the crucible. He'd faced death and found love. He was an adult.

And filled with a quiet fury that would destroy everything in its path. Everything necessary to get to Poppy.

He made other phone calls as he guided the Integra swiftly and expertly through the streets of El Camino. He called the Black Iris and made sure that Ash hadn't turned up there. He called several other black flower clubs, even though he didn't expect to find anything. Poppy had said Ash was going to take her far away.

But where?

Damn you, Ash, he thought. *Where?*

Phil was staring at the TV without really seeing it. How could he be interested in talk shows or infomercials when all he could think about was his sister? His sister who was maybe watching the same shows and maybe out biting people?

He heard the car screech to a stop outside and was on his feet before he knew it. Weird how he was absolutely certain of who it was. He must have come to recognize the Integra's engine.

He opened the door as James reached the porch. "What's up?"

"Come on." James was already heading for the car. There was a deadly energy in his movements, a barely controlled power that Phil had never seen before. White-hot fury, leashed but straining.

"What's *wrong?*"

James turned at the driver's side door. "Poppy's missing!"

Phil threw a wild glance around. There was nobody on the street, but the door to the house was open. And James was shouting as if he didn't care who heard.

Then the words sank in. "What do you mean, she's—" Phil broke off and jerked the door to the house shut. Then he went to the Integra. James already had the passenger door open.

"What do you mean, she's missing?" Phil said as soon as he was in the car.

James gunned the engine. "My cousin Ash has taken her someplace."

"*Who's Ash?*"

"He's dead," James said, and somehow Phillip knew he

didn't mean Ash was one of the walking dead. He meant Ash was going to *be* dead, completely dead, at some point very soon.

"Well, where's he taken her?"

"I don't know," James said through his teeth. "I have no idea."

Phil stared a moment, then said, "Okay. Okay." He didn't understand what was going on, but he could see one thing. James was too angry and too intent on revenge to think logically. He might *seem* rational, but it was stupid to drive around at fifty-five miles an hour through a residential zone with no idea of where to go.

It was strange that Phil felt comparatively calm—it seemed as if he'd spent the last week being wacko while James played the cool part. But having someone else be hysterical always made Phil go levelheaded.

"Okay, look," he said. "Let's take this one step at a time. Slow down, okay? We might be going in exactly the wrong direction." At that, James eased up on the gas pedal slightly.

"Okay, now tell me about Ash. Why's he taking Poppy somewhere? Did he kidnap her?"

"No. He talked her into it. He convinced her that it was dangerous for me if she stuck around here. It was the one thing guaranteed to make her go with him." One hand on the wheel, James fished in his pocket and handed a folded piece of paper to Phil.

It was a page torn out of a book. Phillip read the note and swallowed. He glanced at James, who was staring straight ahead at the road.

Phil shifted, embarrassed at having intruded on private territory, embarrassed at the sting in his eyes. *Your soulmate, Poppy?* Well. Well.

"She loves you a lot," he said finally, awkwardly. "And I'm glad she said goodbye to me." He folded the note carefully and tucked it under the emergency brake handle. James picked it up and put it in his pocket again.

"Ash used her feelings to get her away. Nobody can push buttons and pull strings like he can."

"But why would he want to?"

"First because he likes girls. He's a *real* Don Juan." James glanced at Phil caustically. "And now he's got her alone. And second because he likes to play with things. Like a cat with a mouse. He'll fool around with her for a while, and then when he gets tired of her, he'll hand her over."

Phillip went still. "Who *to?*"

"The Elders. Somebody in charge somewhere who'll realize she's a renegade vampire."

"And then what?"

"And then they kill her."

Phil grabbed the dashboard. "Wait a minute. You're telling me that a cousin of yours is going to hand Poppy over to be killed?"

"It's the law. Any good vampire would do the same. My own mother would do it, without a second thought." His voice was bitter.

"And he's a vampire. Ash," Phil said stupidly.

James gave him a look. "*All* my cousins are vampires," he said with a short laugh. Then his expression changed, and he took his foot off the gas.

"What's the—hey, that was a stop sign!" Phil yelped.

James slammed on the brakes and swung into a U-turn in the middle of the street. He ran over somebody's lawn.

"What is it?" Phil said tightly, still braced against the dashboard.

James was looking almost dreamy. "I've just realized where they've gone. Where he'd take her. He told her someplace safe, where people wouldn't care what she was. But vampires *would* care."

"So they're with humans?"

"No. Ash hates humans. He'd want to take her someplace in the Night World, someplace where he's a big man. And the nearest city that's controlled by the Night World is Las Vegas."

Phil felt his jaw drop. *Las Vegas?* Controlled by the Night World? He had the sudden impulse to laugh. Sure, of course it would be. "And I always thought it was the Mafia," he said.

"It is," James said seriously, swerving onto a freeway on-ramp. "Just a different mafia."

"But, look, wait. Las Vegas is a big city."

"It's not, actually. But it doesn't matter anyway. I know where they are. Because all my cousins *aren't* vampires. Some of them are witches."

Phil's forehead puckered. "Oh, yeah? And how did you arrange that?"

"I didn't. My great-grandparents did, about four hundred years ago. They did a blood-tie ceremony with a witch family. The witches aren't my *real* cousins; they're not related. They're cross-cousins. Adopted family. It probably won't even occur to them that Poppy might not be legal. And that's where Ash would go."

"They're cross-kin," Ash told Poppy. They were driving in the Rasmussens' gold Mercedes, which Ash insisted his aunt Maddy would want him to take. "They won't be suspicious of you. And witches don't know the signs of being a new vampire the way vampires do."

Poppy just stared at the far horizon. It was evening now, and a lowering red sun was setting behind them. All around them was a weird alien landscape: not as brown as Poppy would have expected a desert to be. More gray-green, with clumps of green-gray. The Joshua trees were strangely beautiful, but also the closest thing to a plant made up of tentacles as she'd ever seen.

Most everything growing had spikes.

It was oddly fitting as a place to go into exile. Poppy felt as if she were leaving behind not only her old life, but everything she'd ever found familiar about the earth.

"I'll take care of you," Ash said caressingly.

Poppy didn't even blink.

Phillip first saw Nevada as a line of lights in the darkness ahead. As they got closer to the state line, the lights resolved into signs with blinking, swarming, flashing neon messages. Whiskey Pete's, they announced. Buffalo Bill's. The Prima Donna.

Some guy with a reputation for being a Don Juan was taking Poppy in *this* direction?

"Go faster," he told James as they left the lights behind and entered a dark and featureless desert. "Come on. This car can do ninety."

"Here we are. Las Vegas," Ash said as if making Poppy a present of the whole city. But Poppy didn't see a city, only a light in the clouds ahead like the rising moon. Then, as the freeway curved, she saw that it wasn't the moon, it was the reflection of city lights. Las Vegas was a glittering pool in a flat basin between the mountains.

Something stirred in Poppy despite herself. She'd always wanted to see the world. Faraway places. Exotic lands. And this would have been perfect—if only James had been with her.

Up close, though, the city wasn't quite the gem it looked from a distance. Ash got off the freeway, and Poppy was thrown into a world of color and light and movement—and of tawdry cheapness.

"The Strip," Ash announced. "You know, where all the casinos are. There's no place like it."

"I bet," Poppy said, staring. On one side of her was a towering black pyramid hotel with a huge sphinx in front. Lasers were flashing out of the sphinx's eyes. On the other side was a sleazy motor inn with a sign saying "Rooms $18."

"So this is the Night World," she said, with a twinge of cynical amusement that made her feel very adult.

"Nah, this is for the tourists," Ash said. "But it's good business and you can do some fairly serious partying. I'll show you the real Night World, though. First, I want to check in with my cousins."

Poppy considered telling him that she didn't really care to have *him* show her the Night World. Something about Ash's manner was beginning to bother her. He was acting more as if they were out on a date than as if he were escorting her into exile.

But he's the only person I know here, she realized with a dismayed sinking in her stomach. And it's not as if I have any money or anything—not even eighteen dollars for that crummy motel.

There was something worse. She'd been hungry for some time now, and now she was starting to feel breathless. But she wasn't the dazed, unthinking animal she'd been last night. She didn't *want* to attack some human on the street.

"This is the place," Ash said. It was a side street, dark and not crowded like the Strip. He pulled into an alley. "Okay, just let me see if they're in."

On either side of them were high buildings with cinder-block walls. Above, tiers of power lines obscured the sky. Ash knocked at a door set in the cinder block—a door with no knob on the outside. There was no sign on the door, either, just some crudely spray-painted graffiti. It was a picture of a black dahlia.

Poppy stared at a Dumpster and tried to control her breathing. In, out. Slow and deep. It's okay, there's air. It may not feel like it, but there's air.

The door opened and Ash beckoned to her.

"This is Poppy," Ash said, putting an arm around her as Poppy stumbled inside. The place looked like a shop—a shop with herbs and candles and crystals. And lots of other weird things that Poppy didn't recognize. Witchy-looking supplies.

"And these are my cousins. That's Blaise, and that's Thea." Blaise was a striking girl with masses of dark hair and lots of curves. Thea was slimmer and blond. They both kept going out of focus as Poppy's vision blurred.

"Hi," she said, the longest greeting she could manage.

"Ash, what's wrong with you? She's sick. What have you been doing to her?" Thea was looking at Poppy with sympathetic brown eyes.

"Huh? Nothing," Ash said, looking surprised, as if noticing Poppy's state for the first time. Poppy guessed he wasn't the type to worry about other people's discomfort. "She's hungry, I guess. We'll have to run out and feed—"

"Oh, no, you don't. Not around here. Besides, she's not going to make it," Thea said. "Come on, Poppy, I'll be a donor this once."

She took Poppy by the arm and led her through a bead curtain into another room. Poppy let herself be towed. She couldn't think anymore—and her whole upper jaw was aching. Even the word *feed* sharpened her teeth.

I need . . . I have to . . .

But she didn't know how. She had a vision of her own face in the mirror, silvery eyes and savage canines. She didn't *want* to be an animal again and jump on Thea and rip her throat. And she couldn't ask how—that would give her away as a new vampire for sure. She stood, trembling, unable to move.

CHAPTER 15

"C ome on, it's okay," Thea said. She seemed to be about Poppy's age, but she had a gentle, sensible air that gave her authority. "Sit down. Here." She set Poppy on a shabby couch and extended her wrist. Poppy stared at the wrist for an instant and then remembered.

James, giving her blood from his arm. *That* was how to do it. Friendly and civilized.

She could see pale blue veins under the skin. And that sight blasted away the last of her hesitation. Instinct took over and she grabbed Thea's arm. The next thing she knew she was drinking.

Warm salty-sweetness. Life. Relief from pain. It was so good that Poppy could almost cry. No wonder vampires hated humans, she thought dimly. Humans didn't have to hunt for this marvelous stuff; they were full of it already.

But, another part of her mind pointed out, Thea wasn't

a human. She was a witch. Strange, because her blood tasted exactly the same. Poppy's every sense confirmed it.

So witches are just humans, but humans with special powers, Poppy thought. Interesting.

It took an effort to control herself, to know when to stop. But she did stop. She let go of Thea's wrist and sat back, a little embarrassed, licking her lips and teeth. She didn't want to meet Thea's brown eyes.

It was only then that she realized she'd been keeping her thoughts shielded during the entire process. There had been no mental connection as there had been when she shared blood with James. So she'd mastered one vampire power already. Faster than James or Ash had expected.

And she felt good now. Energetic enough to do the Netherlands skippy dance. Confident enough to smile at Thea.

"Thank you," she said.

Thea smiled back, as if she found Poppy odd or quaint, but nice. She didn't seem suspicious. "It's okay," she said, flexing her wrist and grimacing gently.

For the first time Poppy was able to look around her. This room was more like a living room than part of a shop. Besides the couch there was a TV and several chairs. At the far end was a large table with candles and incense burning.

"This is the teaching room," Thea said. "Grandma does spells here and lets the students hang out."

"And the other part is a store," Poppy said, cautiously because she didn't know what she was supposed to know.

Thea didn't look surprised. "Yes. I know you wouldn't think there'd be enough witches around here to keep us in business, but actually they come from all over the country. Grandma's famous. And her students buy a lot."

Poppy nodded, looking properly impressed. She didn't dare ask more questions, but her chilly heart had warmed just a tiny bit. All Night People weren't harsh and evil. She had the feeling she could be friends with this girl if given the chance. Maybe she could make it in the Night World after all.

"Well, thanks again," she murmured softly.

"Don't mention it. But don't let Ash get you run down like that, either. He's so *irresponsible.*"

"You wound me, Thea. You really do," Ash said. He was standing in the doorway, holding the bead curtain open with one hand. "But come to think of it, I'm feeling a little run down myself. . . ." He raised his eyebrows insinuatingly.

"Go jump in Lake Mead, Ash," Thea said sweetly.

Ash looked innocent and yearning. "Just a little bite. A nibble. A nip," he said. "You have such a pretty white throat. . . ."

"Who does?" Blaise said, pushing her way through the other half of the bead curtain. Poppy had the feeling she was only speaking to focus attention on herself. She stood in the center of the room and shook back her long black hair with the air of a girl used to attention.

"You both do," Ash said gallantly. Then he seemed to remember Poppy. "And, of course, this little dreamer has a pretty white everything."

Blaise, who had been smiling, now looked sour. She stared at Poppy long and hard. With dislike—and something else.

Suspicion. Dawning suspicion.

Poppy could *feel* it. Blaise's thoughts were bright and sharp and malicious, like jagged glass.

Then suddenly Blaise smiled again. She looked at Ash. "I suppose you've come for the party," she said.

"No. What party?"

Blaise sighed in a way that emphasized her low-cut blouse. "The Solstice party, of course. Thierry's giving a big one. *Everybody* will be there."

Ash looked tempted. In the dim light of the teaching room his eyes gleamed dark. Then he shook his head.

"No, can't make it. Sorry. I'm going to show Poppy the town."

"Well, you can do that and still come to the party later. It won't really get going until after midnight." Blaise was staring at Ash with an odd insistence. Ash bit his lip, then shook his head again, smiling.

"Well, maybe," he said. "I'll see how things go."

Poppy knew he was saying more than that. Some unspoken message seemed to be passing between him and Blaise. But it wasn't telepathic, and Poppy couldn't pick it up.

"Well, have a good time," Thea said, and gave Poppy a quick smile as Ash piloted her away.

Ash peered ahead at the Strip. "If we hurry we can watch the volcano erupting," he said. Poppy gave him a look, but didn't ask.

Instead, she said, "What's a Solstice party?"

"Summer solstice. The longest day of the year. It's a holiday for the Night People. Like Groundhog Day for humans."

"Why?"

"Oh, it always has been. It's very magical, you know. I'd take you to the party, but it would be too dangerous. Thierry's a vampire Elder." Then he said, "Here's the volcano."

It was a volcano. In front of a hotel. Waterfalls crashed down its sides, and red lights shone from the cone. Ash double-parked across the street.

"You see, we've got a great view right here," he said. "All the comforts of home."

The volcano was emitting rumbling sounds. As Poppy watched in disbelief, a pillar of fire shot out of the top. Real fire. Then the waterfalls caught fire. Red and gold flames spread down the sides of the black rock until the entire lake around the volcano was ablaze.

"Inspiring, isn't it?" Ash asked, very close to her ear.

"Well—it's . . ."

"Thrilling?" Ash inquired. "Stimulating? Rousing?" His

arm was creeping around her, and his voice was sweetly hypnotic.

Poppy didn't say anything.

"You know," Ash murmured, "you can see a lot better if you get over here. I don't mind crowding." His arm was urging her gently but inevitably closer. His breath ruffled her hair.

Poppy slammed an elbow into his stomach.

"*Hey!*" Ash yelped—in genuine pain, Poppy thought. Good.

He'd dropped his arm and now he was looking at her with aggrieved brown eyes. "What did you do that for?"

"Because I *felt* like it," Poppy said smartly. She was tingling with new blood and ready for a fight. "Look, Ash, I don't know what gave you the idea that I'm your date here. But I'm telling you right now that I'm *not.*"

Ash tilted his head and smiled painfully. "You just don't know me well enough," he offered. "When we get to know each other—"

"*No.* Never. I'm not interested in other guys. If I can't have James . . ." Poppy had to stop and steady her voice. "There's nobody else I want," she said finally, flatly. "Nobody."

"Well, not now, maybe, but—"

"*Never.*" She didn't know how to explain. Then she had an idea. "You know the soulmate principle?"

Ash opened his mouth and then shut it. Opened it again. "Oh, no. Not *that* garbage."

"Yes. James is my soulmate. I'm sorry if it sounds stupid, but it's true."

Ash put a hand to his forehead. Then he started to laugh. "You're serious."

"Yes."

"And that's your final word."

"Yes."

Ash laughed again, sighed, and cast his eyes upward. "Okay. Okay. I should have known." He chuckled in what seemed like self-derision.

Poppy was relieved. She'd been afraid he'd be disgruntled and huffy—or *mean*. Despite his charm, she could always feel something cold running below the surface in Ash, like an icy river.

But now he seemed perfectly good-humored. "Okay," he said. "So if romance isn't on the menu, let's go to the party."

"I thought you said it was too dangerous."

He waved a hand. "That was a little fib. To get you alone, you know." He glanced sideways at her. "Sorry."

Poppy hesitated. She didn't care about a party. But she didn't want to be alone with Ash, either.

"Maybe you should just take me back to your cousins' place."

"They won't *be* there," Ash said. "I'm sure they've gone to the party by now. Oh, come on, it'll be fun. Give me a chance to make things up to you."

Thin curls of uneasiness were roiling inside Poppy. But Ash looked so penitent and persuasive . . . and what other choice did she have?

"Okay," she said finally. "For just a little while."

Ash gave a dazzling smile. "Just a very little while," he said.

"So they could be anywhere on the Strip," James said.

Thea sighed. "I'm sorry. I should have known Ash was up to something. But hijacking your girlfriend . . ." She lifted her hands in a what-next gesture. "For what it's worth, she didn't seem very interested in him. If he's planning to put the moves on her, he's going to get a surprise."

Yes, James thought, and so is she. Poppy was only useful to Ash as long as Ash thought he could play with her. Once he realized he couldn't . . .

He didn't want to think about what would happen then. A quick visit to the nearest Elder, he supposed.

His heart was pounding, and there was a ringing in his ears.

"Did Blaise go with them?" he asked.

"No, she went to the Solstice party. She tried to get Ash to go, but he said he wanted to show Poppy the town." Thea paused, raising a finger. "Wait—you might check at the party. Ash said he might stop in later."

James spent a moment forcing himself to breathe. Then he said, very gently, "And just who is giving this party?"

"Thierry Descouedres. He always has a big one."

"And he's an Elder."

"What?"

"Nothing. Never mind." James backed out of the shop. "Thanks for the help. I'll be in touch."

"James . . ." She looked at him helplessly. "Do you want to come in and sit down? You don't look very well. . . ."

"I'm fine," James said, already out the door.

In the car he said, "You can get up now."

Phillip emerged from the floor of the backseat where he'd been hiding. "What's happening? You were gone a long time."

"I think I know where Poppy is."

"You just *think*?"

"Shut up, Phil." He didn't have energy for exchanging insults. He was entirely focused on Poppy.

"Okay, so where is she?"

James spoke precisely. "She is either now, or she will be later, at a party. A very large party, filled with vampires. And at least one Elder. The perfect place to expose her."

Phil gulped. "And you think that's what Ash is going to do?"

"I know that's what Ash is going to do."

"Then we've got to stop him."

"We may be too late."

The party was strange. Poppy was amazed at how young most of the people were. There were a few scattered adults, but far more teenagers.

"Made vampires," Ash explained obligingly. Poppy remembered what James had said—made vampires remained forever the age of their death, but lamia could stop aging anytime. She supposed that meant that James could get as old as he wanted, while she would be stuck at sixteen eternally. Not that it mattered. If she and James were going to be together, they could both stay young—but apart, maybe he'd want to age.

But it *was* odd to see a guy who looked about nineteen talking earnestly with a little kid who looked about four. The kid was cute, with shiny black hair and tilted eyes, but there was something at once innocent and cruel in his expression.

"Let's see, now that's Circe. A witch of renown. And that's Sekhmet, a shapeshifter. You don't want to get *her* mad," Ash said genially. He and Poppy were standing in a little anteroom, looking down a level into the main room of the house. Of the mansion, rather. It was the most opulent private residence Poppy had ever seen—and she'd seen Bel Air and Beverly Hills.

"Okay," Poppy said, looking in the general direction he was pointing. She saw two tall and lovely girls, but she had no idea which was which.

"And that's Thierry, our host. He's an Elder."

An Elder? The guy Ash was indicating didn't seem older than nineteen. He was beautiful, like all the vampires, tall and blond and pensive. Almost sad-looking.

"How old *is* he?"

"Oh, I forget. He got bitten by an ancestress of mine a long time ago. Back when people lived in caves."

Poppy thought he was joking. But maybe not.

"What do the Elders do, exactly?"

"They just make rules. And see that people keep them." An odd smile was playing around Ash's lips. He turned to look directly at Poppy.

With the black eyes of a snake.

That was when Poppy knew.

She backed away rapidly. But Ash came after her, just as rapidly. She saw a door on the other side of the anteroom and headed for it. Got through it. Only to find herself on a balcony.

With her eyes, she measured the distance to the ground. But before she could make another move, Ash had her arm.

Don't fight yet, her mind counseled desperately. He's strong. Wait for an opportunity.

She made herself relax a fraction and met Ash's dark gaze. "You brought me here."

"Yes."

"To hand me over."

He smiled.

"But *why*?"

Ash threw back his head and laughed. It was lovely, melodious laughter, and it made Poppy sick.

"You're a *human*," he said. "Or you should be. James should never have done what he did."

Poppy's heart was racing, but heir mind was oddly clear. Maybe she'd known all along that this was what he was going to do. Maybe it was even the *right* thing to do. If she couldn't be with James and she couldn't be with her family, did the rest really matter? Did she *want* to live in the Night World if it was full of people like Blaise and Ash?

"So you don't care about James, either," she said. "You're willing to put him in danger to get rid of me."

Ash considered, then grinned. "James can take care of himself," he said.

Which was obviously Ash's entire philosophy. Everybody took care of themselves, and nobody helped anybody else.

"And Blaise knew, too," Poppy said. "She knew what you were going to do and she didn't care."

"Not much gets past Blaise," Ash said. He started to say something else—and Poppy saw her chance.

She kicked—*hard*. And twisted at the same time. Trying to get over the balcony rail.

"Stay here," James said to Phil before the car had even stopped. They were in front of a huge white mansion fringed with palm trees. James threw the door open, but took the time to say again, "Stay *here*. No matter what happens, don't go in that house. And if somebody besides me comes up to the car, drive away."

"But—"

"Just do it, Phil! Unless you want to find out about death firsthand—tonight."

James set out at a dead run for the mansion. He was too intent to really notice the sound of a car door opening behind him.

"And you looked like such a nice girl," Ash gasped. He had both of Poppy's arms behind her back and was trying to get out of the range of her feet. "No—no, quit that, now."

He was too strong. There was nothing Poppy could do. Inch by inch he was dragging her back into the anteroom.

You might as well give up, Poppy's mind told her. It's useless. You're done.

She could picture the whole thing: herself being dragged out in front of all of those sleek and handsome Night People and revealed. She could picture their pitiless eyes. That pensive-looking guy would walk up to her and his face would change and he wouldn't look pensive anymore. He'd look savage. His teeth would grow. His eyes would go silvery. Then he'd snarl— and strike.

And that would be the end of Poppy.

Maybe that wasn't the way they did it, maybe they executed criminals some other way in the Night World. But it wouldn't be pleasant, whatever it was.

And I won't make it easy for you! Poppy thought. She thought it directly at Ash, throwing all of her anger and grief

and betrayal at him. Instinctively. Like a kid shouting in a temper tantrum.

Except it had an effect shouting usually didn't.

Ash flinched. He almost lost his grip on her arms.

It was only a momentary weakening, but it was enough for
Poppy's eyes to widen.

I hurt him. *I hurt him!*

She stopped struggling physically in that same instant. She
put all her concentration, all her energy, into a mental explo-
sion. A thought-bomb.

LET GO OF ME, YOU ROTTEN VAMPIRE CREEP!

Ash staggered. Poppy did it again, this time making her
thought a fire hose, a high-power Jetstream bombardment.

LET GOOOOOOOOOOOO!

Ash let go. Then, as Poppy ran out of steam, he tried in a
fumbling way to reach her again.

"I don't think so," a voice as cold as steel said. Poppy looked
into the anteroom and saw James.

Her heart lurched violently. And then, without consciously
being aware of moving, she was in his arms.

Oh, James, how did you find me?

All he kept saying was, *Are you all right?*

"Yes," Poppy said finally, aloud. It was indescribably good
to be with him again, to be held by him. Like waking up from
a nightmare to see your mother smiling. She buried her face
in his neck.

"You're sure you're all right?"

"Yes. Yes."

"Good. Then just hang on a moment while I kill this guy and we'll go."

He was absolutely serious. Poppy could feel it in his thoughts, in every muscle and sinew of his body. He wanted to murder Ash.

She lifted her head at the sound of Ash's laugh.

"Well, it ought to be a good fight, anyway," Ash said.

No, Poppy thought. Ash was looking silky and dangerous and in a very bad mood. And even if James could beat him, James was going to get hurt. Even if she and James fought him together, there was going to be some damage.

"Let's just go," she said to James. "Quick." She added silently, *I think he wants to keep us around until somebody from the party gets here.*

"No, no," Ash said, in gloatingly enthusiastic tones. "Let's settle this like vampires."

"Let's not," said a breathless familiar voice. Poppy's head jerked around. Climbing over the railing of the balcony, dusty but triumphant, was Phil.

"Don't you *ever* listen?" James said to him.

"Well, well," Ash said. "A human in an Elder's house. What *are* we going to do about that?"

"Look, buddy," Phil said, still breathless, brushing off his hands. "I don't know who you are or what horse you rode in on. But that's my *sister* there you're messing with, and I figure I've got the first right to knock your head off."

There was a pause while Poppy, James, and Ash all looked at him. The pause stretched. Poppy was aware of a sudden, completely inappropriate impulse to laugh. Then she realized that James was fighting desperately not to crack a smile.

Ash just looked Phil up and down, then looked at James sideways.

"Does this guy *understand* about vampires?" he said.

"Oh, yeah," James said blandly.

"And he's going to knock my head in?"

"Yeah," Phil said, and cracked his knuckles. "What's so surprising about that?"

There was another pause. Poppy could feel minute tremors going through James. Choked-back laughter. At last James said, admirably sober, "Phil really feels strongly about his sister."

Ash looked at Phil once more, then at James, and finally at Poppy. "Well . . . there *are* three of you," he said.

"Yes, there are," James said, genuinely sober now. Grim.

"So I guess you do have me at a disadvantage. All right, I give up." He lifted his hands and then dropped them. "Go on, scram. I won't fight."

"And you won't tell on us, either," James said. It wasn't a request.

"I wasn't going to anyway," Ash said. He had on his most innocent and guileless expression. "I know you think I brought

Poppy here to expose her, but I really wasn't going to go through with it. I was just having fun. The whole thing was just a joke."

"Oh, sure," Phil said.

"Don't even bother lying," James said.

But Poppy, oddly, wasn't as certain as they were. She looked at Ash's wide eyes—his wide violet eyes—and felt doubt slosh back and forth inside her.

It was hard to read him, as it had been hard all along. Maybe because he always meant everything he said at the time he said it—or maybe because he *never* meant anything he said. No matter which, he was the most irritating, frustrating, impossible person she'd ever met.

"Okay, we're going now," James said. "We're going to walk very quietly and calmly right through that little room and down the hall, and we're not going to stop for *anything*—Phillip. Unless you'd rather go back down the way you came up," he added.

Phil shook his head. James gathered Poppy in his arm again, but he paused and looked back at Ash.

"You know, you've never really cared about anyone," he said. "But someday you will, and it's going to hurt. It's going to hurt—a lot."

Ash looked back at him, and Poppy could read nothing in his ever-changing eyes. But just as James turned again, he said, "I think you're a lousy prophet. But your girlfriend's a good one. You might want to ask her about her dreams sometime."

James stopped. He frowned. "What?"

"And you, little dreamer, you might want to check out your family tree. You have a very loud yell." He smiled at Poppy engagingly. "Bye now."

James stayed for another minute or so, just staring at his cousin. Ash gazed serenely back. Poppy counted heartbeats while the two of them stood motionless.

Then James shook himself slightly and turned Poppy toward the anteroom. Phil followed right on their heels.

They walked out of the house very quietly and very calmly. No one tried to stop them.

But Poppy didn't feel safe until they were on the road.

"What did he mean with that crack about the family tree?" Phil asked from the backseat.

James gave him an odd look, but answered with a question. "Phil, how did you know where to find Poppy in that house? Did you see her on the balcony?"

"No, I just followed the shouting."

Poppy turned around to look at him.

James said, "What shouting?"

"*The* shouting. Poppy shouting. 'Let go of me, you rotten vampire creep.'"

Poppy turned to James. "Should *he* have been able to hear it? I thought I was just yelling at Ash. Did everybody at the party hear?"

"No."

"But, then—"

James cut her off. "What dream was Ash talking about?"

"Just a dream I had," Poppy said, bewildered. "I dreamed about him before I actually met him."

James's expression was now *very* peculiar. "Oh, did you?"

"Yes. James, what's this all about? What did he mean, I should check my family tree?"

"He meant that you—and Phil—aren't human after all. Somewhere among your ancestors there's a witch."

CHAPTER 16

You have *got* to be kidding," Poppy said.

Phil just gaped.

"No. I'm perfectly serious. You're witches of the second kind. Remember what I told you?"

"There are the kind of witches that know their heritage and get trained—and the kind that don't. Who just have powers. And humans call that kind—"

"Psychics!" James chorused with her. "Telepaths. Clairvoyants," he went on alone. There was something in his voice between laughing and crying. "Poppy, that's what *you* are. That's why you picked up on telepathy so quickly. That's why you had clairvoyant dreams."

"And that's why Phil heard me," Poppy said.

"Oh, no," Phil said. "Not me. Come on."

"Phil, you're twins," James said. "You have the same ancestors. Face it, you're a witch. That's why I couldn't control your mind."

"Oh, *no*," Phil said. "No." He flopped back in his seat. "No," he said again, but more weakly.

"But whose side do we get it from?" Poppy wondered.

"Dad's. Of course." The voice from the backseat was very faint.

"Well, that would *seem* logical, but—"

"It's the truth. Don't you remember how Dad was always talking about seeing weird things? Having dreams about things before they happened? And, Poppy, he heard you yell in *your* dream. When you were calling for James. James heard it, and I heard it, and Dad heard it, too."

"Then that settles it. Oh, and it explains other things about all of us—all those times we've had *feelings* about things—hunches, whatever. Even you have hunches, Phil."

"I had one that James was creepy, and I was right."

"Phil—"

"And maybe a few others," Phil said fatalistically. "I knew it was James driving up this afternoon. I thought I just had a fine ear for car engines."

Poppy was shivering with delight and astonishment, but she couldn't quite understand James. James was absolutely beaming. Filled with unbelieving elation that she could feel like streamers and fireworks in the air. "What, James?"

"Poppy, don't you see?" James actually pounded the steering wheel in joy. "It means that even before you became a vampire, *you were a Night Person. A secret witch.* You have every right to know about the Night World. You belong there."

The world turned upside down and Poppy couldn't breathe. At last she whispered. "Oh . . ."

"And we belong together. Nobody can separate us. We don't have to hide."

"Oh . . ." Poppy whispered again. Then she said, "James, pull the car over. I want to kiss you."

When they were in motion once more, Phil said, "But where are you two going to go now? Poppy can't come home."

"I know," Poppy said softly. She had accepted that. There was no going back for her; the old life was over. Nothing to do but build a new one.

"And you can't just wander around from place to place," Phil said, doggedly persistent.

"We won't," Poppy said calmly. "We'll go to Dad."

It was perfect. Poppy could feel James think, *Of course.*

They would go to her father, the always-late, always-impractical, always-affectionate parent. Her father the witch who didn't know he was a witch. Who probably thought he was crazy when his powers acted up.

He'd give them a place to stay, and that was all they needed, really. That and each other. The whole Night World would be open to them, whenever they wanted to explore it. Maybe they could come back and visit Thea sometime. Maybe they could dance at one of Thierry's parties.

"If we can *find* Dad, that is," Poppy said, struck by sudden alarm.

"You can," Phil said. "He flew out last night, but he left an address. For the first time."

"Maybe somehow he knew," James said.

They rode for a while, and then Phil cleared his throat and said, "You know, I just had a thought. I don't want any part of the Night World, you understand—I don't *care* what my heritage is. I just want to live like a human—and I want everybody to be clear on that. . . ."

"We're clear, Phil," James interrupted. "Believe me. Nobody in the Night World is going to force you in. You can live like a human all you want as long as you avoid Night People and keep your mouth shut."

"Okay. Good. But here's my thought. I still don't approve of vampires, but it occurs to me that maybe they're not as completely bad as they seem. I mean, vampires don't treat their food any worse than humans do. When you think of what we do to cows . . . at least they don't breed humans in pens."

"I wouldn't bet on it," James said, suddenly grim. "I've heard rumors about the old days. . . ."

"You always have to argue, don't you? But my other thought was that you're part of Nature, and Nature just is what it is. It's not always pretty, but . . . well, it's Nature, and there it is." He wound up glumly, "Maybe that doesn't make any sense."

"It makes sense to me," James said, entirely serious.

"And—thanks." He paused to look back at Phil in acknowledgment. Poppy felt a sting behind her eyes. If he admits we're part of Nature, she thought, then he doesn't believe we're unnatural anymore.

It meant a lot.

She said, "Well, you know, *I've* been thinking, too. And it occurs to me that maybe there are other choices for feeding besides just jumping on humans when they don't expect it. Like animals. I mean, is there any reason their blood won't work?"

"It's not the same as human blood," James said. "But it's a possibility. I've fed on animals. Deer are good. Rabbits are okay. Possums stink."

"And then there must be *some* people who'd be willing donors. Thea was a donor for me. We could ask other witches."

"Maybe," James said. He grinned suddenly. "I knew a witch back home who was *very* willing. Name of Gisèle. But you couldn't ask them to do it every day, you know. You'd have to give them time to recover."

"I know, but maybe we could alternate. Animals one day and witches the next. Hey, maybe even werewolves on weekends!"

"I'd rather bite a possum," James said.

Poppy socked him in the arm. "The point is, maybe we don't have to be horrible bloodsucking monsters. Maybe we can be *decent* bloodsucking monsters."

"Maybe," James said quietly, almost wistfully.

"Hear, hear," Phil said very seriously from the back.

"And we can do it together," Poppy said to James. He took his eyes off the road to smile at her. And there was nothing wistful about his gaze. Nothing cool or mysterious or secretive, either.

"Together," he said out loud. And mentally he added, *I can't wait. With that telepathy of yours—you realize what we can do, don't you?*

Poppy stared, then felt an effervescent rush that almost shot her out of the car. *Oh, James—do you think?*

I'm certain. The only thing that makes exchanging blood so special is that it enhances telepathy. But you *don't need any enhancement—you little dreamer.*

Poppy sat back to try and still her heart.

They would be able to join their minds again. Anytime they wanted. She could imagine it, being swept into James's mind, feeling him surrender his thoughts to hers.

Merging like two drops of water. Together in a way that humans could never know.

I can't wait, either, she told him. *I think I'm going to like being a witch.*

Phil cleared his throat. "If you guys want some privacy . . ."

"We can't have any," James said. "Not with you around. Obviously."

"I can't help it," Phil said through his teeth. "You're the ones who're yelling."

NIGHT WORLD

"We're not yelling. You're snooping."

"Both of you give it a rest," Poppy said. But she felt warm and glowing all over. She couldn't resist adding to Phil, "So, if you're willing to give us some privacy, that means you trust James alone with your sister. . . ."

"I didn't *say* that."

"You didn't have to," Poppy said.

She was happy.

It was very late the next day. Almost midnight, in fact. The witching hour. Poppy was standing in a place she'd thought she'd never see again, her mother's bedroom.

James was waiting outside with a carload of stuff, including one large suitcase of Poppy's CDs, smuggled for them by Phil. In a few minutes James and Poppy would be heading for the East Coast and Poppy's father.

But first, there was something Poppy had to do.

She glided quietly toward the king-size bed, making no more noise than a shadow, not disturbing either of the sleepers. She stopped by her mother's still form.

She stood looking down, and then she spoke with her mind.

I know you think this is a dream, Mom. I know you don't believe in spirits. But I had to tell you that I'm all right. I'm all right, and I'm happy, and even if you don't understand, please try to believe. Just this once, believe in what you can't see.

She paused, then added, *I love you, Mom. I always will.*

When she left the room, her mother was still asleep—and smiling.

Outside, Phil was standing by the Integra. Poppy hugged him and he hugged back, hard.

"Goodbye," she whispered. She got into the car.

James stuck his hand out the window toward Phil. Phil took it without hesitation.

"Thank you," James said. "For everything."

"No, thank *you*," Phil said. His smile and his voice were both shaky. "Take care of her . . . and of yourself." He stepped back, blinking.

Poppy blew him a kiss. Then she and James drove off together into the night.

The Night World lives on in *Daughters of Darkness*, by L. J. Smith.

R owan, Kestrel, and Jade," Mary-Lynnette said as she and Mark passed the old Victorian farmhouse. "Huh?"

"Rowan. And Kestrel. And Jade. The names of the girls who're moving in." Mary-Lynnette tilted her head toward the farmhouse—her hands were full of lawn chair. "They're Mrs. Burdock's nieces. Don't you remember I told you they were coming to live with her?"

"Vaguely," Mark said, readjusting the weight of the tele-scope he was carrying as they trudged up the manzanita-covered hill. He spoke shortly, which Mary-Lynnette knew meant he was feeling shy.

"They're pretty names," she said. "And they must be sweet girls, because Mrs. Burdock said so."

"Mrs. Burdock is crazy."

"She's just eccentric. And yesterday she told me her nieces

are all beautiful. I mean, I'm sure she's prejudiced and every-thing, but she was pretty definite. Each one of them gorgeous, each one a completely different type."

"So they should be going to California," Mark said in an almost-inaudible mutter. "They should be posing for *Vogue*. Where do you want this thing?" he added as they reached the top of the hill.

"Right here." Mary-Lynnette put the lawn chair down. She scraped some dirt away with her foot so the telescope would sit evenly. Then she said casually, "You know, I thought maybe we could go over there tomorrow and introduce ourselves—sort of welcome them, you know. . . ."

"Will you cut it *out*?" Mark said tersely. "I can organize my own life. If I want to meet a girl, I'll meet a girl. I don't need help."

"Okay, okay. You don't need help. Be careful with that focuser tube—"

"And besides, what are we going to say?" Mark said, on a roll now. "'Welcome to Briar Creek, where nothing ever hap-pens. Where there are more coyotes than people. Where if you *really* want some excitement you can ride into town and watch the Saturday night mouse racing at the Gold Creek Bar. . . .'"

"Okay. Okay." Mary-Lynnette sighed. She looked at her younger brother, who just at the moment was illuminated by the last rays of sunset. To see him now, you'd think he'd never been sick a day in his life. His hair was as dark and shiny as

Mary-Lynnette's, his eyes were as blue and clear and snapping. He had the same healthy tan as she did; the same glow of color in his cheeks.

But when he'd been a baby, he'd been thin and scrawny and every breath had been a challenge. His asthma had been so bad he'd spent most of his second year in an oxygen tent, fighting to stay alive. Mary-Lynnette, a year and a half older, had wondered every day if her baby brother would ever come home.

It had changed him, being alone in that tent where even their mother couldn't touch him. When he came out he was shy and clingy—holding on to their mother's arm all the time. And for years he hadn't been able to go out for sports like the other kids. That was all a long time ago—Mark was going to be a junior in high school this year—but he was still shy. And when he got defensive, he bit people's heads off.

Mary-Lynnette wished one of the new girls *would* be right for him, draw him out a bit, give him confidence. Maybe she could arrange it somehow. . . .

"What are you thinking about?" Mark asked suspiciously.

Mary-Lynnette realized he was staring at her.

"About how the seeing's going to be really good tonight," she said blandly. "August's the best month for starwatching; the air's so warm and still. Hey, there's the first star—you can make a wish."

She pointed to a bright point of light above the southern horizon. It worked; Mark was distracted and looked, too.

Mary-Lynnette stared at the back of his dark head. If it would do any good, I'd wish for romance for you, she thought.

I'd wish it for myself, too—but what would be the point? There's nobody around here to be romantic *with*.

None of the guys at school—except maybe Jeremy Lovett—understood why she was interested in astronomy, or what she felt about the stars. Most of the time Mary-Lynnette didn't care—but occasionally she felt a vague ache in her chest. A longing to . . . share. If she *had* wished, it would have been for that, for someone to share the night with.

Oh, well. It didn't help to dwell on it. And besides, although she didn't want to tell Mark, what they were wishing on was the planet Jupiter, and not a star at all.

Mark shook his head as he tramped down the path that wound through buckbrush and poison hemlock. He should have apologized to Mary-Lynnette before leaving—he didn't *like* being nasty to her. In fact, she was the one person he usually tried to be decent to.

But why was she always trying to *fix* him? To the point of wishing on stars. And Mark hadn't really made a wish, anyway. He'd thought, if I was making a wish, which I'm not because it's hokey and stupid, it would be for some excitement around here.

Something wild, Mark thought—and felt an inner shiver as he hiked downhill in the gathering darkness.

Jade stared at the steady, brilliant point of light above the southern horizon. It was a planet, she knew. For the last two nights she'd seen it moving across the sky, accompanied by tiny pinpricks of light that must be its moons. Where she came from, nobody was in the habit of wishing on stars, but this planet seemed like a friend—a traveler, just like her. As Jade watched it tonight, she felt a sort of concentration of hope rise inside her. *Almost* a wish.

Jade had to admit that they weren't off to a very promising start. The night air was too quiet; there wasn't the faintest sound of a car coming. She was tired and worried and beginning to be very, very hungry.

Jade turned to look at her sisters.

"Well, where *is* she?"

"I don't know," Rowan said in her most doggedly gentle voice. "Be patient."

"Well, maybe we should scan for her."

"No," Rowan said. "Absolutely not. Remember what we decided."

"She's probably forgotten we were coming," Kestrel said. "I told you she was getting senile."

"Don't *say* things like that. It's not *polite*," Rowan said, still gentle, but through her teeth.

Rowan was always gentle when she could manage it. She was nineteen, tall, slim, and stately. She had cinnamon-brown eyes and warm brown hair that cascaded down her back in waves.

Kestrel was seventeen and had hair the color of old gold sweeping back from her face like a bird's wings. Her eyes were amber and hawklike, and she was never gentle.

Jade was the youngest, just turned sixteen, and she didn't look like either of her sisters. She had white-blond hair that she used as a veil to hide behind, and green eyes. People said she looked serene, but she almost never felt serene. Usually she was either madly excited or madly anxious and confused.

Right now it was anxious. She was worried about her battered, half-century-old Morocco leather suitcase. She couldn't hear a thing from inside it.

"Hey, why don't you two go down the road a little way and see if she's coming?"

Her sisters looked back at her. There were few things that Rowan and Kestrel agreed on, but Jade was one of them. She could see that they were about to team up against her.

"Now what?" Kestrel said, her teeth showing just briefly.

And Rowan said, "You're up to something. What are you up to, Jade?"

Jade smoothed her thoughts and her face out and just looked at them artlessly. She hoped.

They stared back for a few minutes, then looked at each

other, giving up. "We're going to have to walk, you know," Kestrel said to Rowan.

"There are worse things than walking," Rowan said. She pushed a stray wisp of chestnut-colored hair off her forehead and looked around the bus station—which consisted of a three-sided, glass-walled cubicle, and the splintering wooden bench. "I wish there was a telephone."

"Well, there isn't. And it's twenty miles to Briar Creek," Kestrel said, golden eyes glinting with a kind of grim enjoyment. "We should probably leave our bags here."

Alarm tingled through Jade. "No, *no*. I've got all my—all my clothes in there. Come on, twenty miles isn't so far." With one hand she picked up her cat carrier—it was homemade, just boards and wires—and with the other she picked up the suitcase. She got quite a distance down the road before she heard the crunch of gravel behind her. They were following: Rowan sighing patiently, Kestrel chuckling softly, her hair shining like old gold in the starlight.

The one-lane road was dark and deserted. But not entirely silent—there were dozens of tiny night sounds, all adding up to one intricate, harmonizing night stillness. It would have been pleasant, except that Jade's suitcase seemed to get heavier with every step, and she was hungrier than she had ever been before. She knew better than to mention it to Rowan, but it made her feel confused and weak.

Just when she was beginning to think she would have to

put the suitcase down and rest, she heard a new sound.

It was a car, coming from behind them. The engine was so loud that it seemed to take a long time to get close to them, but when it passed, Jade saw that it was actually going very fast. Then there was a rattling of gravel and the car stopped. It backed up and Jade saw a boy looking through the window at her.

There was another boy in the passenger seat. Jade looked at them curiously.

They seemed to be about Rowan's age, and they were both deeply tanned. The one in the driver's seat had blond hair and looked as if he hadn't washed in a while. The other one had brown hair. He was wearing a vest with no shirt underneath. He had a toothpick in his mouth.

They both looked back at Jade, seeming just as curious as she was. Then the driver's window slid down. Jade was fascinated by how quickly it went.

"Need a ride?" the driver said, with an oddly bright smile. His teeth shone in contrast to his dingy face.

Jade looked at Rowan and Kestrel, who were just catching up. Kestrel said nothing, but looked at the car through narrow, heavy-lashed amber eyes. Rowan's brown eyes were very warm.

"We sure would," she said, smiling. Then, doubtfully, "But we're going to Burdock Farm. It may be out of your way. . . ."

"Oh, hey, I know that place. It's not far," the one in the vest said around his toothpick. "Anyway, anything for a lady," he said, with what seemed to be an attempt at gallantry. He opened his door and got out of the car. "One of you can sit up front, and I can sit in back with the other two. Lucky me, huh?" he said to the driver.

"Lucky you," the driver said, smiling largely again. He opened his door, too. "You go on and put that cat carrier in front, and the suitcases can go in the trunk," he said.

Rowan smiled at Jade, and Jade knew what she was thinking. *I wonder if everybody out here is so friendly?* They distributed their belongings and then piled in the car, Jade in the front with the driver, Rowan and Kestrel in the back on either side of the vested guy. A minute later they were flying down the road at what Jade found a delightful speed, gravel crunching beneath the tires.

"I'm Vic," the driver said.

"I'm Todd," the vested guy said.

Rowan said, "I'm Rowan, and this is Kestrel. That's Jade up there."

"You girls friends?"

"We're sisters," Jade said.

"You don't look like sisters."

"Everybody says that." Jade meant everybody they had met since they'd run away. Back home, everybody *knew* they were sisters, so nobody said it.

"What are you doing out here so late?" Vic asked. "It's not the place for nice girls."

"We're not nice girls," Kestrel explained absently.

"We're *trying* to be," Rowan said reprovingly through her teeth. To Vic, she said, "We were waiting for our great-aunt Opal to pick us up at the bus stop, but she didn't come. We're going to live at Burdock Farm."

"Old lady Burdock is your aunt?" Todd said, removing his toothpick. "That crazy old bat?" Vic turned around to look at him, and they both laughed and shook their heads.

Jade looked away from Vic. She stared down at the cat carrier, listening for the little squeaking noises that meant Tiggy was awake.

She felt just slightly . . . uneasy. She sensed something. Even though these guys seemed friendly, there was something beneath the surface. But she was too sleepy—and too light-headed from hunger—to figure out exactly what it was.

They seemed to drive a long time before Vic spoke again.

"You girls ever been to Oregon before?"

Jade blinked and murmured a negative.

"It's got some pretty lonely places," Vic said. "Out here, for example. Briar Creek was a gold rush town, but when the gold ran out and the railroad passed it by, it just died. Now the wilderness is taking it back."

His tone was significant, but Jade didn't understand what he was trying to convey.

"It does seem peaceful," Rowan said politely from the backseat.

Vic made a brief snorting sound. "Yeah, well, peaceful wasn't exactly what I meant. I meant, take this road. These farmhouses are miles apart, right? If you screamed, there wouldn't be anyone to hear you."

Jade blinked. What a strange thing to say.

Rowan, still politely making conversation, said, "Well, you and Todd would."

"I mean, nobody *else*," Vic said, and Jade could feel his impatience. He had been driving more and more slowly. Now he pulled the car off to the side of the road and stopped. Parked.

"Nobody out *there* is going to hear," he clarified, turning around to look into the backseat. Jade looked, too, and saw Todd grinning, a wide bright grin with teeth clenched on his toothpick.

"That's right," Todd said. "You're out here alone with us, so maybe you'd better listen to us, huh?"

Jade saw that he was gripping Rowan's arm with one hand and Kestrel's wrist with the other.

Rowan was still looking polite and puzzled, but Kestrel looked at the car door on her side thoughtfully. Jade knew what she was looking for—a handle. There wasn't one.

"Too bad," Vic said. "This car's a real junkheap; you can't even open the back doors from inside."

He grabbed Jade's upper arm so hard she could feel pressure on the bone. "Now, you girls just be nice and nobody's going to get hurt."